The Mexican

Frank Nester is a small time criminal who manages to pull off an almost faultless railroad robbery, except for a burnt hand when he grips a stovepipe to steady himself. This injury points to his presence in the mail car and sees him taken into custody. But luck is on his side and the jury finds him not guilty, much to the annoyance of special agent Rodney D. Dodd. So when an almost exact duplication of the robbery occurs two years later for a haul of cash that is nearly forty times greater, Dodd sets his sights on Frank. However, this crime includes a killing. A Mexican jeweller by the name of Don DeLuca, who was travelling in the first class compartment, was hit by a stray shot. Dodd says it's murder and that Frank should hang. Frank knows he had nothing to do with the heist. So who did? And what has happened to the body of Don DeLuca?

By the same author

Raking Hell
No Coward
The Proclaimers
Reaper
Reins of Satan

For more information about
the author's other books, please visit:
www.leeclinton.com

The Mexican

Lee Clinton

A Black Horse Western
ROBERT HALE

ISBN 978-0-7198-2015-1

The Crowood Press
The Stable Block
Crowood Lane
Ramsbury
Marlborough
Wiltshire SN8 2HR

www.crowood.com

Robert Hale is an imprint
of The Crowood Press

Typeset by Catherine Williams, Knebworth

Printed and bound in Great Britain by
CPI Antony Rowe, Chippenham and Eastbourne

For Joanne W.
Girls write Westerns too.

1

THE SPRING HILL HEIST

1885, Stilwell, Kansas

The robbery of the 10:05 from Stilwell had been as slick as bacon grease. Or so said Special Agent Rodney D. Dodd of the Missouri Pacific Railroad Police Department in his report. He wrote of how two masked outlaws had jumped aboard the moving train from their galloping mounts just as the locomotive pulled hard up the Spring Hill incline. On that day the 10:05 comprised of three passenger cars; four flatbeds stacked heavy with steel track reclaimed from the decommissioned Tulsa spur line to Muskogee; and a mail van positioned to the rear.

The criminals then climbed to the top of the van and entered through the roof ventilation port, catching the mail clerk completely by surprise as he dozed from the warmth of the stove. The report went on to say that under the threat of a thrashing from the burly brutes, the portly clerk reluctantly unlocked the safe. The amount taken from the cash box was stated to be $2,573.58, which was tipped into an empty mailbag and tied tight for carrying. It was noted that the thieves were quick and proficient in their unlawful act. The clerk estimated that they took no more than five minutes from entry to when they jumped with their plunder from the car's rear platform. This timing allowed them to alight just before the crest of Spring Hill, where the train was travelling at its slowest speed, and at a blind bend that hid any inadvertent observation by the passengers or crew.

No one was injured in the stunt, except for a burn to the left hand of one of the outlaws. It seemed that he had mistakenly gripped the flue from the van's potbelly stove where it vented from the roof, to steady himself as he prepared to enter through the ventilation port. The guard observed the red burn marks when the thief wrapped a blue bandana around his palm as a bandage. Still, it had not hindered his movements or ability to finish the job.

It was this wound that led to the would-be culprit's capture two days later when drinking, with the use of his good hand, at the Silver Dollar Saloon on Fourth Avenue, Emporia. He was returned to Stilwell for trial with the expectation of a guilty verdict. However, his explanation as to the cause of the injury, along with his confident manner and the timidness of the mail clerk to make a positive identification, led the jury to find the accused, Francis T. Nester, innocent and he walked free.

Not one penny of the stolen money, which had come from the profits of stock sales at the McAlester Cattle Yards, was recovered. The Cattlemen's Association quickly claimed reimbursement from the Missouri Pacific Railroad who was responsible for the security of cash and valuables during transportation. MPR in turn claimed indemnity from their insurers, Kansas Industrial.

While some in the community saw the whole shebang as a victimless crime, it was not how Agent Dodd viewed the matter. In a statement of the obvious, made in his report's summation, he said that theft was still theft and at the end of the day, it was commerce and the community who ended up paying for the loss of revenue. He then went on to positively identify Frank Nester as one of the three men involved, as Dodd had concluded that an additional man had been used to muster and handle the horses during the heist. The special agent also gave Frank a backhanded compliment by saying that while it was a malicious crime, it had been planned and executed with meticulous skill.

Finally, Dodd, who had once served in the New Orleans Police Department, stated that Nester was a lifelong felon and would re-offend. In his closing verdict he said that when he did, he would be caught and made to pay in full. This was no idle boast. Dodd was known to get his man, but not always within the confines of the law. A point that had been noted, yet quietly tolerated by his superiors via the turning of a blind eye.

2

MURDER

1887, Stilwell, Kansas

The second Spring Hill heist was practically a mirror reflection of the first, just two years apart and almost to the day. Special Agent Dodd was again the investigator and stated that the two robberies shared the same *modus operandi*. He liked to use Latin to impress, but why he just couldn't say that they were similar in execution was beyond his superiors. However, Dodd now saw himself as a man in the public eye and this led to a sense of self-importance and bravado. Other railway employees held a different opinion, with the station agent at Cold Water Springs calling the special agent an insufferable pain in the rear end on more than one occasion.

Maybe someone else, a little higher up in the Missouri Pacific, should have also tossed some additional criticism in Dodd's direction as his report was incorrect in at least two aspects of the robbery. The first was the amount taken, which was some forty times more than the original theft, amounting to nearly $100,500. This vast sum had once again come from the McAlester cattle yards, which led some to say that lightning had not only struck the livestock yards twice, but this time with forty bolts of fury. It was a wry reflection that was not lost on the Kansas Industrial Insurance office, who still retained the contract as the insurers of the Missouri Pacific Railroad.

The second incorrect deduction by Dodd was that this heist had been as slick as the first. In fact, it had the hallmark of being somewhat clumsy, as a wayward warning shot had been fired that resulted in the death of a passenger who sat alone in the only first class compartment, which was hitched to the mail car. The shot was not heard above the noise of the train by any of the second or third class passengers and the fatality was only discovered on arrival of the train in Kansas City. He was a Mexican businessman by the name of Don DeLuca.

Gossip as to who was responsible was rife when news of the train robbery made it into the papers and the illustrated magazines. Then in no time at all the *Stilwell Chronicle* announced in bold headlines DODD GETS HIS MAN. It made for great copy and the man was Frank Nester, but some readers thought this was a little premature as Frank had only been charged and not yet convicted, let alone sentenced. However, it was true that he was being held behind bars and the charges were serious, even if the comparisons of the two crimes seemed rather odd, and as time would tell, somewhat suspicious.

Frank was well known throughout Johnson County as a bit of a rogue who had come from a family of scoundrels on his father's side. Mostly their misdeeds were based around thieving but never directly from neighbours or those down on their luck. His mother was an altogether different kettle of fish. She was an educated woman who had met and married Frank's father at Fort Scott. 'It must have been the uniform,' was a common comment made by those seeking to understand the attraction, as the two seemed to have little in common. She was refined, while her husband was rough.

Frank was the spit from his father's mouth in both looks and manner. He was muscular but not burly, athletic but not sporty, compact but not short. He could also be abrupt, often rude and occasionally disrespectful. If wronged he could be mean, yet surprisingly, he remained well-mannered and courteous in the company of women and was careful with his language. But amongst men he would not be bullied and returned like with like, being both abrasive and threatening. This all seemed to stem from a heightened level of confidence in his abilities, along with a disposition that did not take to fools. Essentially, these were the immature characteristics of a cocky youth. However, Frank was now twenty-seven years of age.

When just a lad, his schoolteacher Miss Briscoe had high hopes for Frank Junior at the Number 3 Johnson County Public School; she saw him as bright and capable with words and numbers. Yet the family ties that bind had quickly taken him down 'the lower road of life'. It was a term Miss Briscoe re-used again in her comments to her older brother on seeing the headlines in the newspaper.

The first Spring Hill heist had given Frank some unwanted criminal notoriety, but locals eventually decided to give him the benefit of the doubt in regards to guilt or innocence. The common belief was that if he had done it, then why wasn't he living high off the hog? After all, that haul two years ago represented five years' pay for an enterprising family with working sons, yet he showed no extravagance in any form. As for this second heist, which had resulted in his arrest, it was at a much different level of wrongdoing altogether, and one, which on the surface at least, made no sense.

Firstly, what would any man, let alone Frank, do with over $100,000? Could anyone in Johnson County spend such a sum in a lifetime? And secondly, their Frank wouldn't go around firing off chaotic shots. Yes, he carried a gun, a Smith & Wesson No. 3 revolver, but it hardly ever left its old cavalry holster on his waist belt as fists were his first choice of weapons. In fact, the whole circumstances surrounding the incident seemed somewhat peculiar, and to call it murder was puzzling in the least. Just one single shot had been fired and the bullet had passed through the door panel of the mail van, then through the wall of the first class car to strike the seated passenger in the back.

An accident most would claim, but not Special Agent Dodd. He said publicly before the trial had even begun, in his oddly pitched voice and Louisiana accent (which some-times sounded shrill and even childlike) that had Frank not pulled this second railroad robbery, then Mr Don DeLuca would still be alive and in the loving bosom of his family. He went on to argue that it was Frank Nester who had started a sequence of criminal events, which resulted in the instant and untimely death of a fine and decent man, as surely as if Frank had put the gun to the passenger's head and shot him in cold premeditated murder. Dodd was developing a way with long-winded orations that some thought would better serve a career on the stage.

Further south at the McAlester Cattlemen's Association, the question most asked was, why had such a large sum of money been transported at one time? It represented some six to eight months of trading. And why after the experience of having lost revenue under similar circumstances some two years prior? As for the charge of murder, would it stick in a court of law? Some cattlemen said no, while those who took a more jaundiced view of the quality of jurymen in Johnson County thought that it just might. And this possibility raised the other intriguing question, that of the deceased. Just who was Don DeLuca?

Little was known about him, other than he was travelling alone and seemed to be well-heeled. He was dressed in a smart three-piece cotton twill suit and travelling on a first class ticket from Shreveport to Kansas City. Surprisingly, however, he had no luggage and only one form of identifica-tion, a single business card in his wallet stating that he was a jeweller and gold broker from across the Rio Grande at Reynosa, who specialized in ornaments and trinkets of pre-cious metals and gems.

His body was returned to his native Mexico with haste,

yet no recording of an obituary was reported in the local press from south of the border. In fact, it was as if Don DeLuca had disappeared immediately after the tragic event. The only explanation given for this urgent vanishing act was a questioning belief that maybe this was the custom of Mexicans when dealing with their dead. This then became an often-repeated comment in Stilwell gossip that finally transformed into fact. But for whatever reasons, the body of Don DeLuca had gone, and not that long after, was forgotten.

3

THE TRIAL

Stilwell Town Hall

The trial of Frank Nester was set to open before the county circuit judge and a jury of twelve. The court location was moved by the clerk of the court, from the old courthouse on Floyd Street to the town hall, to accommodate the expected interest from the locals. Stilwell had not seen such a shebang in ages. The headlines of the *Chronicle* on the commencement of proceedings read LET THE TRIAL BEGIN. It was, if nothing else, dramatic. What was to follow was also somewhat theatrical, which could best be described as a trumped-up charade that served neither justice nor the law.

Frank swore his innocence to his family, especially his mother, while Dodd pronounced that Francis T. Nester was guilty to anyone who would listen to his annoying squeaky voice. Frank had unwisely dismissed Dodd as a fool and had publicly referred to him as Nelly, which was a none-too-subtle slight not just on the pitch of his voice but also his overall manliness. But now, for both of them, it was their day in court and all eyes were on Frank when the clerk asked him to stand.

'Does the accused plead guilty or not guilty?'

The court reporter, a young man on his first assignment for the *Stilwell Chronicle* sat upright and tall to observe the dishevelled accused who sported a week old growth.

'Of course I'm not guilty, you idiot,' came the reply. 'I didn't do any of it. Either robbing or shooting.'

It was the Frank Nester that everyone knew and in response the gallery laughed. The judge, Chester Millbrook, looked up with displeasure and clenching the head of his gavel, jabbed the handle towards the accused to make his point. 'Just answer the question and refrain from calling the clerk of the court an idiot, or I will have you removed from the proceedings.'

The court reporter caught the indignant look on Frank's face as he responded. 'Removed from the proceedings to where?'

'Back to the cells, that's where.'

The astonishment remained. 'How can I defend myself from the cells?'

The judge's tone now became mocking. 'You will be represented by your legal counsel, that's how.'

'What legal counsel?'

'The legal counsel provided by the court, who has been allocated to defend you, that's who.'

'Where? I can't see him.'

The judge became a little contrite. 'Well, he has to get here from Topeka and he's running late.'

Any possible sense of atonement by Frank now evaporated like drops of rain upon a hot branding iron. He couldn't believe what he was hearing.

'But,' continued the judge, 'there is no need to stop proceedings just because he's not here yet. Clerk, please record the plea of not guilty. Let the trial begin. Prosecutor Jenkins, you may start.'

'Yes, judge.'

Jenkins, like Dodd, was in the pay of the Missouri Pacific Railroad and mostly dealt with the acquisition of land under the property laws. He was urbane, ambitious, and had an eye on a political career with the Democrats. This criminal case, he hoped, would be the lily pad on which to hop over to the other side of the legal-political swamp.

'Gentlemen of the jury, you have before you a man accused of a murderous crime.' He paused for effect. 'The killing of an innocent.' Another pause. 'A person from Mexico who had travelled north to our fair vistas for commerce.' Jenkins now pulled on the lapels of his coat and raised his voice. 'And I will present to you evidence that he was shot dead by this man.' He pointed at Frank. 'While committing a callous crime to enrich himself on other people's money. And gentlemen.' His voice was now softer. 'I want you to keep this in mind, that had you been sitting in that carriage, in that particular seat, on that fateful day, minding your own business and thinking of your loved ones at home, then it would be you, not Mr Don DeLuca, for whom this trial is now seeking justice.'

'Hogwash,' called Frank aloud. 'None of them have ever travelled first class in their lives.'

Laughter erupted from the gallery.

'Quiet,' shouted the judge. 'The accused has been warned. Any more and a charge of contempt will be laid.'

Frank went to reply then decided it was best to hold his tongue.

'Continue, Prosecutor Jenkins.'

Jenkins gave a small bow. 'May I now call on the first witness, Mr Samuel Davidson?'

On cue the judge called, 'Mr Samuel Davidson is so called.'

'Samuel Davidson, calling Samuel Davidson,' shouted the clerk in a voice as if delivering a telegram to a guest in a hotel lobby.

Sam Davidson entered the court from the side vestibule of the town hall. He was sworn in and identified himself as an employee of the Missouri Pacific Railroad and the mail clerk on duty on the day of the robbery. However, mail clerking was not his normal job. In fact, he worked as a wages clerk in the Legal Department of the Missouri Pacific and had been allocated the role of mail clerk at short notice as a fill-in. This detail was volunteered by a nervous Davidson as a defence should he be questioned on the precise duties required of a mail clerk. None of this, however, made any impact on Frank, who had never seen the man before in his life. Or if he had, he had clearly forgotten, which would not be hard to do as Sam Davidson was a nondescript man, a little overweight, starting to bald, and with weak eyes that seemed to require spectacles.

As Davidson began to quickly recite the events of that day he started to perspire.

'He came in through the ceiling vent,' he said with excitement. 'On his own, jumping to the floor as I attended

17

to my obligations. "Hold up," he said and brandished a pistol in my face. I stood fast and refused to cower. He threatened again, then ,,,' Davidson wrinkled his brow. '… he became flustered. "I'll kill you dead", he said.'

Frank couldn't contain himself. 'No one says that,' he called out. '"I'll kill you dead". And I've never been flustered in my life.' It was a mock that some in the court who knew Frank well, tended to agree with.

'Silence,' called the judge.

Frank held his tongue and the murmur of the audience went quiet.

'Continue. What was said next?'

Davidson took in a breath. '"Watch," cried the criminal. "I will fire a shot to show you I mean business." "Where?" I asked. "Through that door," he said, pointing towards the first class carriage. "Not there," said I—'

'Said I?' repeated Frank under his breath in ridicule.

'"It is the first class compartment," I pleaded, "and you will put some poor innocent in danger".'

The gallery was now transfixed upon the testimony of Davidson as he spoke.

'"I care not," he replied and fired.' Davidson slapped the arm of the chair in which he was seated for effect. The audience gasped. 'And judge, you know the rest.'

'Indeed I do,' said the judge while nodding his head.

Frank couldn't believe what he was hearing, and repeated with sarcasm the words, 'I care not,' just as his eye caught the wide smile on 'Nelly' Dodd's face. He then looked with contempt at Davidson who was now sweating profusely.

Prosecutor Jenkins put the question. 'And did you see the perpetrator of these crimes?'

'I did, when his blue bandana was blown from his face

by the wind as he alighted from the moving train with the haul.'

'And do you see him now?'

Davidson paused then stammered as he squinted at Frank. 'I do.'

'And who is that man?'

Samuel Davidson pointed to Frank. 'The accused.'

The gallery gasped as one then broke into a loud but inaudible conversation, while Frank shook his head and called for someone to give Davidson a telescope as he was clearly as blind as a bat.

Meanwhile, the court reporter remained silent and kept his eyes on Frank, for it was the manner of the accused that caught his interest. Here was a man with clear contempt of both the court and the circumstances he faced. Here, he thought, was a genuine rough man of the Old West. A type he had read about when in college in the East while studying. At last, he thought with intense joy, I am seeing a true outlaw, one just like Jesse James. This is a man of the ilk of the wild cowboy and the brawling fist fighter, horse thief and bank robber. He drew in an excited breath. A genuine gunslinger and a killer.

It is true that most young men from the East, especially those of a bookish nature, tended to let their imaginations run wild when travelling West; and this junior newspaper reporter was no different. Hopefully, his editor would keep him in check when he got to see the elaborate copy that his cadet was about to turn in. But then again, judging from recent headlines by his editor, maybe not.

4

THE ATTORNEY

Later in the day

The defence attorney arrived on the 2:15 from Kansas City, having missed the 9:05. He collected his bag, booked into the Traveller's Rest Boarding House before strolling across to the Crown Saloon for a quick stiffener on the way to the courthouse. From there he was directed to the Town Hall, but he stopped once again at a saloon for a second charge. He finally arrived just as the judge called an end to the first day of the trial and eventually got to sit down with his client at 4:35.

'Where the hell have you been?' Frank's greeting said it all, in regard to his infuriation.

'Delayed by destiny, my boy. But here I am now to serve at your pleasure and at no cost. So go gentle on complaints of punctuality.'

Frank was less than impressed. 'No cost? I've never heard of a free lawyer,' he said. 'Someone's got to pay!'

'Quite so, but not you. The state pays me a small stipendiary, but hardly enough to cover amenities. You could almost call my services *pro bono publico*.'

Frank detected a slight slur in the speech and looked at the flushed cheeks of the attorney before leaning in and taking a sniff. 'You've been drinking. I can smell it on you.'

'Just a tot.'

'A top up, more like.'

'Every man has a vice. Mine is a little drink or two. What's yours?' The attorney smiled. 'Other than breaking the law, robbing mail vans and killing innocent people.'

Frank rocked back in his chair. 'You hold on a minute, I haven't killed anyone, up to now.'

'The law said you did.' The attorney's eyebrows rose, as if correcting a child who had just told a fib.

'I'm innocent,' protested Frank.

'Ah, they all say that. Even I will say that, on your behalf.' The attorney smiled with stained teeth just before his breath hit Frank full in his face.

Frank grimaced as he leant back in his chair. 'You're supposed to save me.'

'No, I'm here to defend you. Saving requires additional expenses.' The attorney rubbed the middle finger against his thumb. 'Anyway, that may all be too late now. To buy off the judge would be difficult. That is always best done before you get to court, during preliminary proceedings. You should have called me earlier.'

'I didn't even know you existed until today.'

The attorney conceded to Frank's observation. 'Of course, but here I am now, Fletcher Prowse, attorney of law, in your servitude.'

'Frank Nester, your client,' was the mocking reply.

No hand was extended or received by either party in greeting.

'Nes-ter or Nes-tor?' Prowse enunciated slowly.

'Nes-ter,' mimicked Frank. Then without taking a breath, said, 'How are you going to get me justice?'

Fletcher Prowse raised his eyes to the ceiling. 'Oh, justice, justice, justice.' It was said as if he were about to start a soliloquy to an audience.

Frank was not in the mood for theatrics. 'Yeah, justice.'

Prowse seemed to become instantly weary and slumped back in his chair while tucking his thumbs into the fob pockets of his waistcoat.

'Justice may come to you in the next life, but certainly not in this one. Here, all you get is the law.'

'What's the difference?' Frank was genuinely confused.

'One gives you fairness, while the other gives you a ruling. Nothing more and nothing less.'

'Are you telling me I won't get a fair trial?'

'No such thing, my boy. Even if the twelve men of the jury give you the benefit of the doubt, someone will think that you are guilty. In this particular case the family and friends of Mr Don DeLuca, who would think it exceedingly unfair if you walked free.' Prowse clicked his tongue on the pronunciation of the surname DeLuca.

Frank slapped the surface of the small table between them with his open hand. 'I don't care what his family think, because I didn't do it. Got it?'

Prowse showed no sign of surprise at the emotion or the eruption. 'Got it. But it makes no difference if you did it or not. The law can still find you guilty.'

'Well then, the law is a—' Frank stopped abruptly as he searched for the word.

'An idiot, so I believe the saying goes,' offered the attorney.

'Yeah, that's what I was about to say. An idiot.'

'Someone said it before you.'

'Who?' asked Frank, showing his innocent curiosity.

'Oliver Twist.'

'Who?'

'It is from *The Adventures of Oliver Twist*. No matter. The issue at hand is this: you are on hard times, my little Dorrit, so don't expect too much. But first things first. Tell me about your past crimes.'

Frank was just about to start when he paused before saying, 'Why does that matter? I haven't committed this one.'

'Perhaps not, but maybe for your past sins you are now expected to be punished. To square the books. Some would say that is justice.'

'I'll tell you what justice is, having me walk free.'

'What? To commit new crimes?'

'To do what I want when I want, that's what. Besides, everything is legal if you don't get caught.'

'How profound,' said Fletcher Prowse. 'I'll have to write that one down for my memoirs. However, the reality is that none of us can do what we want when we want. Not even President Cleveland. We are all bound by bonds and conventions, including yours truly. And my bond at the moment is to save you from the gallows.'

'That's something they won't be able to stick on me,' said Frank.

The look on the attorney's face said different.

Frank fell silent before he finally said, 'But I didn't do it. I've done other things, but I've never killed anybody in my life.' He dropped his head. 'Dodd is out to get me. Like you said, to square the books.'

Fletcher Prowse sat and observed the young man before him without saying a word, and despite all the faults that this attorney had accumulated over some forty or more years of legal practice, he was by both nature and training a good judge of character. His instincts told him that on this particular point his client was indeed honest, and therefore innocent of the charges that had been laid upon him.

'We will have to think smart,' he murmured. 'Murder can

be hard to beat in this neck of the woods. Especially when railway men and cattle owners are involved and smell blood. We may have to compromise.'

Frank leaned in. 'What does that mean?'

'It means horse trading, and at the moment we don't have much to trade with.'

Frank was despondent and dropped his head.

'What are you like at trusting people?'

Frank looked up. 'Why?'

'You are going to have to trust me to work in your best interests, even when it doesn't look that way.'

'Do I have a choice?' asked Frank.

'Probably not.'

'So what does it matter?'

The attorney looked concerned. 'It matters in that we will both have to live with the consequences of my efforts, be they good, bad or indifferent. However, failure for me will just cause further professional embarrassment to an already damaged reputation. But for you it could be much, much worse.'

5

IN A PICKLE

The next two days

If the first day of the trial was one of theatre, then the second and third days were that of vaudeville. But Frank was neither entertained nor amused. He felt numb and concerned, a little like an exhausted man who knew that it was dangerous to fall asleep. It was similar to the feeling he had experienced when running stolen horses out of the state for three days straight, without rest, and in fear of being chased down and caught. Only this time he had been caught.

It was now becoming apparent to Frank that whatever sense the judge and jury were making of the evidence being put before them, none of it was in his favour. And as for some of the assumptions and details being provided by the prosecutor, it was as if Jenkins had been involved in the heist himself. Frank thought all of this to be so fanciful that he wondered if a crystal ball was going to be produced. It was such a concocted story as to be both bizarre and foolish. However, the look on the faces of the public in the gallery was one of acceptance and this disheartened Frank enormously, making him fall into a mood that was halfway between desperation and a sulk.

Attorney Prowse said little so Frank drew the conclusion that he was clueless as to how to address the wrongs that were being trotted out in a continuous barrage against him. Frank's destiny now seemed to fall completely upon the jury and trying to read them was impossible. To pass the time he racked his brains to determine if he had ever stolen directly or indirectly from any of the jurors who now held his fate in their hands. His final conclusions were not good, especially if it also included their kinfolk by marriage. So, he consoled himself with the thought that they were only minor misdemeanours and mostly conducted years ago when just a youth, or sort of youthful.

If there was a bright light at all to this dark situation, it was that the talk of murder had stopped and turned to where the stolen money might be. Certainly Frank didn't know, so it was no good asking him. He didn't even know where the original takings from the first heist were. By a most unfortunate turn of events, the money, which had been placed in a mailbag for ease of carriage, had been buried in a place without the knowledge of Frank or his partner in crime, Ned Wilson. As Dodd had correctly assumed in his report on the first heist, there had been a third accomplice. His name was Todd Lennon, a fourteen-year-old boy who was living at home with his mother. Young Todd was recruited on the quiet, out of earshot of his mother, specifically for this job after Ned had noticed his superior horse handling skills. Todd rounded up the mounts as soon as Frank and Ned had climbed onto the mail van. He then galloped the three horses through the woods, out of sight of the train, up to the top of the incline where he waited to receive the mailbag full of cash and hand back the horses to Frank and Ned.

This excellent plan then went askew. Frank and Ned separated and rode hard to pre-arranged locations where they could be seen in public to support their alibis. Todd rode up into the hills with the sack of cash and a shovel, and buried it near Little Peak. The plan was coming together well, but when Todd was less than a mile from the safety of his home, bad luck struck and things went terribly wrong. He was thrown forward from his horse when crossing the ford at Turtle Creek. His mount had stepped into an unseen crevice midstream that snapped the front left leg, causing it to fall and tumble. The stream was not deep, but Todd hit the top of his head upon the rocky bottom from the violent toss, and ended up face down in the water, unconscious. In less than five minutes he had drowned. A neighbour found the wet and lifeless body not more than ten minutes later and being unable to revive the boy, draped him over his horse and walked the body to his mother's small farm. The shock caused Sarah Lennon, a handsome woman of thirty-four years, to withdraw into a deep and abiding silence. Ned felt such guilt over the whole affair that he visited her almost daily, to do the chores that Todd would have done had he still been alive.

Frank and Ned spent hours, days, weeks and months looking for that buried treasure, and although the search continued with obsession, they couldn't find a trace. Their young companion had done such a thorough job of conceal-ment that only he knew of its whereabouts. Frank tried to think through every possibility of where the mailbag might be buried to the point where it had been giving him both dyspepsia and insomnia. Ned meanwhile became solemn and disheartened as fifteen per cent of the haul was owing to Todd and he wanted to give this to Sarah, as well as another fifteen per cent from his share to compensate for his guilt.

'We are in a pickle,' said Prowse when he saw Frank that evening.

The attorney had turned up late again and Frank could smell him before he saw him.

'The saloon still has another hour of trading so what are you doing here?' came Frank's caustic greeting.

Prowse treated the remark like water upon a duck's back. 'I was seeking knowledge.'

'Yeah,' said Frank with palpable disrespect. 'And what did you learn?'

'That the drinkers think you are guilty, of sorts.'

'Of sorts?'

'The sorts that say, on balance, you were probably

involved and good luck to you with the haul, but you shouldn't have killed an innocent passenger, even if he was a Mexican and you didn't mean to.' Fletcher Prowse paused before saying, 'They are an accommodating lot, the men of Stilwell, but there is also a touch of envy, too. Envy that you may be able to live like a prince for the rest of your life on the proceeds of the crime.'

'Envy? I'm in jail. I'm on trial. There's talk of murder. Where do these people get their thinking from?'

''Tis but human nature, my boy.'

'It's liquor talk.' Frank began to shake his head. 'So does it really matter what they think?'

'Yes, I think it does.'

'They're not the jury.'

'True, but I bet the jury are thinking just like their neighbours in the saloon. Or do you have faith in their judgement to make you a free man?'

'No. I've been stitched up.'

'I think you have, too, and by someone who is both smart and lucky. You've made it easy for them as you don't have an alibi.'

'I had no need. I wasn't there, I didn't do it, remember?'

'So where were you again?'

'With Ned.'

'Doing what?'

'Digging holes.'

'Why?'

'Don't ask.'

'And nobody saw you?'

Frank just shook his head in silence.

The attorney looked up at the ceiling and scratched under his chin. 'Anyway, the issue of you being set up will have to be addressed later. We now need to prepare an alternate plan to our primary course of action.'

'Alternate? I didn't know we had any plan at all,' said Frank before pleading his innocence again. 'I didn't do it.' But it came out more like a mournful mumble than a statement of fact.

'Guilt or innocence matters not at the moment. We have to minimize the damage and start trading. At the moment it is shaping up to just two alternatives.'

'And they are?' asked Frank.

'Do I need to spell them out to you, my boy? They are either a rope or a life sentence.'

Frank grimaced. 'I've never killed a man in my life.'

'So you keep saying.' The attorney continued. 'Mind you, these alternatives are just legal opinions. However, we must not let them become a reality.'

'So what is this alternative plan of yours?'

The attorney became businesslike, spreading the fingers of both hands palm down on the table between them.

'The Missouri Pacific Railroad wants a conviction. It's good for business. Restores confidence to their customers, and I dare say the McAlester Cattlemen's Association want a conviction, too. It all helps with the finalisation of the insurance claim.' The middle finger lifted on his right hand as if a signal that an important point was about to be announced. 'But it is the State of Kansas that wants your hide most of all.' Frank's partly inebriated lawyer lowered his finger. 'Well, not necessarily your hide, any hide will appease a politician, but yours is the only one available at the moment.'

Frank had now closed his eyes and dropped his chin to his chest.

The attorney stopped talking.

'I'm listening,' said Frank as he opened his eyes slowly. 'I was just wondering if I'd wake up and all this would go away.'

'I'm afraid not,' said the lawyer in a matter of fact manner. 'Robberies committed on the public way, especially large ones, are not good for community confidence when it comes to travel. Nor for voting back incumbents in an election, and one is coming up soon. Both the Democrats and the Republicans are all about law and order at the moment and keeping life pure. Why, there's even talk that they are going to enforce the prohibition laws. Can you believe that?'

'So where does that leave me?' asked Frank.

'In a pickle jar, right near the bottom.' Both middle fingers of the lawyer's hands lifted this time. 'I need to pluck you from the bottom and at least get you near the top of the jar without getting my hand caught.' Fletcher Prowse twisted his mouth in thought. 'This is going to be tricky, though.'

Frank sat and watched in silent thought, then said, 'So what is this pickle jar plan of yours?'

'You plead guilty. But not before we do some plea bargaining.'

'Is that it?'

'Yes, I know it is something of a shock, but it will allow us to save you from the noose and reduce your sentence. Because guilty or innocent, the system has their man, you, and they want a conviction.'

Frank seemed to slump in the chair. 'How long? How long will I have to spend inside?'

'If this plan works, I'd say, normally, twenty to twenty-five years.'

Frank slumped further down in his chair.

'But I say we be bold in our negotiations with the judge and the prosecutor by playing a full hand that shows every loose end in this case for what it is – fraudulent.'

Frank was unimpressed. He felt like a heavy weight was pressing down on his chest and was about to tip him back off his chair and drive him through the floor.

'So what can you get it down to?'

'Don't know. Anything under twenty is a winning hand. Anything under fifteen is a royal flush.'

'You make it sound like a game of cards.'

'That's what it is, my boy. A game, a gamble, a risk.'

Frank pulled himself up a little. 'Can you do it?'

The attorney rubbed his chin. 'I used to be able to, once, when I was a smart young lawyer, and not in the grip of the grape.'

'But what about now?'

Attorney Prowse looked Frank directly in the eye. 'Now? Now that I'm a broken down old legal hack and a drunkard?'

Frank nodded. 'Yes, now.'

'I don't know. If I get this wrong, you could swing at the end of a rope.'

Prowse started to fidget and Frank noticed. It was a nervous mannerism. He'd seen similar in his partner, Ned, just before a job.

'If I were to spend twenty years locked up, then I'd rather be dead,' said Frank. 'Fifteen is borderline. Anything under that and I will have some life to live when I get out. Fifteen years and I'll be forty-two. My father was dead at fifty-three and I've been living his life over. That would leave me with eleven years. It's not much but at least it's double figures.'

The lawyer shrugged. 'You are a most practical man, Frank Nester, and my pathetic plan is not worthy of such pragmatism,' he said with gloom. 'But I feel we have no choice.'

Frank had resigned himself to the reality. 'I know when I'm done for, and I trust you to do your best. Fifteen and I'll do a deal, although this is going to kill my mother.'

'Is she not well?'

'No, she is fine of body, but I have disappointed her beyond the pale and broken her heart often.' Frank sounded truly remorseful.

'I understand,' said Fletcher Prowse in agreement. 'Maybe if you explained to her the circumstances of your innocence?'

'It would do no good. She warned me that it would come to this but I refused to listen. Besides, would she believe me? I've lied to her so many times before.'

'Is there anyone to care for her?'

'My older brothers, Robert and Albert will see her right. They will also stay close to home and be more careful from here on in after what has happened to me. And I have no doubt that they will all be better off without me.'

'Francis. You see life as it is, not as it should be, and maybe that's what makes you who you are, both smart and likeable.'

Frank looked up at the attorney with a weak smile. 'A rascal much like yourself, eh?'

The lawyer gave some thought to what Frank had just said and smiled back. 'I'll take that as a compliment, my boy. Gracious praise from someone with the credentials to know. A fellow rascal.'

6

THE BARGAIN

The next morning

'Lilac? Who's smelling like lilac in my chamber?' The judge was in an aggravated mood.

'It was provided to me by the madam of my boarding house,' explained Attorney Fletcher Prowse.

'In God's name, why?'

'She said men are wearing it on the European continent.'

'That's no excuse. This is Kansas. Next you'll be putting jojoba oil in your hair.'

Prosecutor Jenkins laughed to humour the judge.

The judge ignored the sycophantic gesture. 'Well, come on, Fletcher, you called this parlay, so get on with it. What have you got on offer? I'm sure Richard is keen to hear.'

'Not really,' corrected Richard Jenkins. 'Your man is guilty and I will prove it. I see no need for discussion. He may plea, but I don't have to listen.'

The arrogance of the prosecutor made Prowse smile. He could smell hubris, and like pride, he always believed that it came before a fall.

'Ah, but can you prove it to the satisfaction of the jury?' he said. 'Sitting in judgement of a neighbour can come with its own peculiarities. They have known my client since he was a nipper, and local gossip, as I hear it, gives him the benefit of the doubt.' Fletcher knew it wasn't so, but he saw the fib as a professional necessity if he was to get Frank his deal. 'And say just by chance that you don't get a guilty verdict. How will that be seen in certain partisan circles?' This was a pointed reference to Jenkins's own political ambitions, which were linked to the success of this case.

The judge's eyebrow elevated slightly and confirmed to Fletcher Prowse that his comment had hit the mark.

'I will persuade the jury beyond doubt, believe me.' Prosecutor Jenkins was being both defiant and pompous. He got up as if to leave.

'Hold on. Let Fletcher have his say,' said the judge. 'You never know, he may be changing his client's plea to guilty.'

'That's precisely what I am proposing,' said Prowse.

'In return for what?' asked Jenkins with suspicion.

'A reduced sentence, of course.'

'Reduced to what?'

'Ten years.'

'Ten years,' Jenkins scoffed. 'The only reduction I'll agree to is the length of the rope.'

'You'll never get a hanging sentence.' Fletcher Prowse spoke slowly.

The judge bristled. 'If he's found guilty, that's my business, not yours, Fletcher.'

'What I meant, Judge, is that Richard will not be able to prove murder. Maybe involuntary manslaughter, but I even doubt that, too.'

'How so?' asked Richard Jenkins, pointing his chin in Prowse's direction.

'You don't have a body. No *corpus de-lic-ti*.' The attorney's tongue clicked on the middle syllable.

'Of course not, the deceased was returned to his loved ones in Mexico.'

'With haste?'

'It is the Mexican way.'

'So they say. But any movement of a body has to conform to both federal and State laws. And you have no certificate of death.'

'Yes, I have.'

'Then show me.'

Jenkins was a little hesitant. 'Well, not with me, but I'll get one.'

'From where – Mexico? Because I asked to see a copy before I left Kansas City. It was the reason why I was delayed. There is no record of the death of Mr Don DeLuca on the state records. No record at all.'

'Then I'll send to Mexico for one.'

'No, you won't,' said the judge. 'This court is in session and it's not going to suspend for weeks or months while you look for a death certificate somewhere in Mexico.' The judge deliberated for a moment. 'Not sure if I could accept it anyway. Kansas authorities should have raised one before they released the body.'

'That, Judge, is precisely the problem. The body wasn't released. I checked,' said Attorney Prowse.

'What do you mean?' The judge was looking serious.

'Well, as best as I can make out, from my enquiries in Kansas City and Topeka, the body was taken direct to the Union Depot after the killing.'

'Yes, that is my understanding,' said the judge. 'Aboard the same train on which he had been travelling when he was killed.'

'But from there the body was handed over to a third party, who it is said, immediately took it to a Missouri under-taker who prepared the deceased for shipment.' Frank's attorney had their undivided attention. 'And, whoever that representative was, he had Mr Don DeLuca on a train bound for San Antonio the following morning, early.'

'That is fast,' said the judge.

'Slick, even,' confirmed Prowse. 'So when we go back into court, I'm going to call for the certificate of death and by doing so, let the cat out of the bag.'

Jenkins protested. 'I'll get an affidavit from the undertaker.'

Fletcher Prowse cut him short. 'Which undertaker? No one seems to know. Strange, isn't it? But there is even a more pressing issue, and this is one for the Missouri Pacific Railroad, your employer.' He was now looking directly at Jenkins. 'They shipped the body of the deceased south without seeing the death certificate first, which is in breach of the law.'

Jenkins knew the implications immediately and went a little pale. If this information was known publicly it would not reflect well on the company he worked for, and his superiors would not be pleased.

The judge got the drift. 'OK, let's put away the rope. You've won that round. But what about the money? That is a twenty-five year sentence if ever I've seen one. Unless he's going to give it back! And all of it.'

'No,' said Prowse. 'He can't. He hasn't got it. Frank is a petty thief, not someone with a mind for grand larceny. And what would he do with such an amount of over $100,000?'

'But I say he has got it, somewhere,' said Jenkins boldly.

'But got what precisely? The money taken from the safe in the mail van, which was then placed into a mail sack?'

'Yes. Precisely that. The money.' Jenkins was trying to sound confident with his confirmation.

'Do you know how much $100,000 weighs?'

'Weighs? What has that got to do with anything?'

'This. Your man, Sam Davidson, the would-be mail clerk but really a wages clerk in your department, said in his written statement, which I have read in detail several times, that the thief threw the mail bag, with all the money in it, over his shoulder and leapt from the moving train and departed on foot at a swift pace.'

'Yes. Is that a problem?' The question showed Jenkins's doubt in taking anything at face value any more.

'The Agricultural Bank has told me that such an amount in small notes, which is the usual currency of a cattle yard, would weigh over 200 pounds. If true, how any man could jump from a moving train with such a weight in a sack and remain on his feet and run swiftly away is beyond me. But I'm happy to put it to the test for the jury. All you need to do is select a man of the same size and weight as Frank. Then we can get him to jump from a moving van down at the station with the same size and weight in a sack, while over his shoulder of course. But I would also get the town doctor to come along as well as he may have to splint a broken leg or two.'

'OK, OK, Fletcher, you've made your point,' said the judge. 'No need for amusement.'

'No, Judge, quite right.' Prowse was suitably contrite. He had just fired off his best shot and it had hit its target. Now was not the time to offend Judge Chester Millbrook's sensibilities.

The judge turned to the prosecutor. 'What do you want to do, Richard?' he asked.

'These are technicalities. I say he's still guilty,' replied the prosecutor.

'Debatable,' said the judge. 'What I want to know is what will you accept on behalf of your client, the Missouri Pacific

Railroad and the co-aggrieved, the McAlester Cattlemen's Association? If it is nothing, then we go back into court and you put your evidence to the jury.'

'Ten is too low, at least fifteen years,' said Jenkins.

'Fletcher?' said the judge, looking for a response.

'No, Judge, Frank won't accept fifteen and I agree with him. He is being generous in offering to do ten. However, I do understand Richard's predicament, and I would accept twelve on Frank's behalf.'

The prosecutor wiped a trembling hand over his brow. He had not seen this coming. 'Only if there is no parole period,' he said, more as a request than a statement.

Fletcher's heart lifted. He had won the day. 'I suppose,' he said slowly, 'I could get my client to accept that.'

'Done then,' said the judge. 'It's a bargain and a satisfactory conclusion for all parties.'

It was a moot point, thought Fletcher, twelve years is still a long time, but at least it has to be better than swinging from the end of a rope.

7

RELEASE

1899 Kansas State Penitentiary, Lansing

The dogs were barking – one of their own was being let off the chain. Frank was going home and the tin cups were rattling against the bars of Cell Block E in celebration. He had done his time and paid his dues, so said Warden

Thompson when he shook Frank's hand. But number 4657 Frances T. Nester didn't need to be reminded that he had served out every day of his twelve year sentence, with no parole, no leniency, no nothing.

Frank stood quietly, listening to the standard, slick and shallow speech of a public official who only allowed himself to get close to a prisoner on the day of their release.

'It is now time to start a new life,' announced Thompson.

'Yes, sir,' said Frank. 'That's exactly what I intend to do, start a new life.'

Even today, Frank was playing the game he'd been forced to live for the last twelve years. It was a game of survival. Keep your nose clean, and never, never show defiance to those with power, be it guard or prisoner.

'Good,' responded Thompson, as if his affirmation could make it so, while Frank silently clutched at his few personal possessions wrapped in newspaper, a luxury denied for the past twelve years. 'I don't ever want to see you back here again, Frank.'

'No way, sir, not me, I've learnt my lesson.'

Thompson smiled. 'Good boy, Frank. Then it is a worthwhile lesson that has been well learnt.'

Frank looked at Warden Thompson and wanted to ask what was that worthwhile lesson, precisely? Was it the daily grind of the relentless work details; or the monotony of the endless repetitive routine; or the sameness of the meagre tasteless ration; or maybe it was the unjustified brutality of sadistic guards? Or was it just the turning of a blind eye to a fight between prisoners, when three attack one? Exactly what was this worthwhile lesson, warden? Being locked up for a crime when innocent? But Frank knew not to ask now or ever, and Thompson turned and walked away.

The two guards who had escorted Frank down to the front gate unlocked the small final door set within the larger solid timber gate. Oh, how he had dared to dream of this moment, every night, and now it was finally here. He watched the door open to freedom with a sense of disbelief.

'See you, Frank,' came the final farewell from one of the guards.

'No, you won't,' said Frank as he stepped over the stoop and into the chilly early morning sunlight as a free man. The trap door closed behind him with a cold thud. Frank looked back up at the imposing bleak structure with its tall double gates. 'I'll tell you what I learnt, warden,' he said aloud with anger, addressing the fortress, 'I learnt that it's not about the crime; it's only about getting caught. That's what I learnt.' He went to turn but stopped. 'And I tell you what else I learnt. If you don't want to get caught, set up some goat like me who everybody thinks is guilty; that's what I learnt. Well, I've learnt the lesson, up here.' Frank pointed to the side of his head then prodded a finger against his skull, just below where the clippers had cut his dark hair back to the bone. 'I'm going to make sure I don't get caught, ever again. That's what I learnt. Because I ain't ever going back inside, for nobody.'

'Frank, how you doing?' The voice was soft and apologetic.

Frank turned and looked at the man who had appeared as if from nowhere and he didn't recognize him.

'It's me, Ned.'

Frank squinted a little. 'Ned?'

'Yeah, Ned. I came up to meet you. How are you doing, Frank?'

'Oh, I'm just fine and dandy. Twelve years down the

drain. I couldn't be better.' It was said with a mix of rage and sarcasm. Frank then paused and looked at Ned. 'You've not been well?'

'No, I'm fine, sort of.'

'You don't look fine.'

'Just older, that's all. And it's my teeth. I lost some teeth, it makes me look …' Ned paused. 'But you look good, Frank.'

Frank studied Ned and observed the rough and worn state of his clothes. 'Things tough, Ned?'

Ned just gave a nod.

'And you came up to meet me today?'

'Yeah.'

'Been waiting long?'

'Every day. I counted down every day.'

Frank kept his eyes on Ned. 'No, I mean, since you got here?'

'Got here last night.'

'Last night? Where did you sleep?'

'Up against the wall. I wanted to make sure I didn't miss you.'

Frank felt his pent-up fury start to fade. It was replaced with a feeling of gratitude towards his old partner, and it was a reaction he hadn't felt in years. He didn't expect anyone to meet him, not even his brothers, but Ned had come. Ned, his companion from all those years ago. He tucked his newspaper-wrapped possessions under his arm and stepped up to Ned and gave him a brotherly embrace.

'It was a cold night last night,' he said.

'Yeah, but I was OK, when I got out of the wind.'

Frank felt the boniness of Ned's frame before releasing his grip. 'I thought I was lean. You need a good feed, Ned.'

Ned smiled in response, showing where three front teeth

were missing. 'Sarah is putting on a spread.'

'Sarah?'

'Sarah Lennon. I'm with Sarah Lennon now.'

'What? Married?'

'No, not married, just together, but permanent like.'

'Oh,' Frank said before nodding his approval. 'Good to be with someone. Todd's mother, right? Sarah Lennon.'

'Yeah, Todd's mother. You want to go?' asked Ned.

'Yeah, I want to go,' said Frank, giving a glance over his shoulder at the giant prison doors before spitting on the ground.

Together the two old friends walked away, side by side, down to the tracks, before running the last hundred yards to catch up to a freight train pulling empty flatbeds towards the Kansas City junction. From there they jumped a string of boxcars heading south and found that they were travelling with three homeless brothers.

'You going to Tulsa Junction?' one of them asked.

'No,' Ned told them, 'only down to Stilwell.'

The bigger of the hobos looked at Frank with his newspaper-wrapped parcel on his lap and asked with a smart mouth, 'You just get out then?'

Ned shifted uneasily as he prepared for trouble.

'Yeah,' said Frank without flinching. 'Today.'

'What were you in for?'

Frank looked the mouth in the eye and said with firm ease, 'Killing.'

The response had its clout and the fellow travellers shut up for the rest of the journey.

When Ned and Frank finally arrived at the Lennons' property, it was just before last light. The lines of the homestead and small barn were much as Frank remembered, except that once he got close, he could see that it was in need of repair, having to step over a hole on the weather beaten porch. Yet, the yard looked neat and the fruit trees down the side were well tended.

When Sarah gave him a hug and a kiss to the cheek Frank was taken by surprise. He had not felt the tenderness of a woman's touch in twelve years, and his response showed. His arms hung limp by his side and he stumbled over his greeting. Then when she smiled at him with warmth in the soft light of the small front room, Frank felt a pang of guilt for not having gone to her son's funeral. Ned had attended while Frank had spent the day digging holes up on Little Peak searching for the money Todd had buried. The young boy had deserved better. She had deserved better, he thought with embarrassment and now here she is inviting me in for supper.

The spread that was laid before them was by no means a banquet, but to Frank it was a superb meal of boiled chicken, gravy, potatoes, peas and cornbread. He was about three parts through this little feast when he realized that Ned was eating little and Sarah even less. He paused, as the understanding of his own stupidity hit home. This was all they had and here he was devouring the lion's share like a glutton.

He put down his spoon, still full of gravy, and said, 'I've never eaten so well, but I couldn't fit in another scrap. You've filled me up like a boot.' Frank saw Sarah's eyes light up as she gazed upon his unfinished meal.

'Eat up, Frank, it's all for you,' said Ned.

'No,' said Frank, 'I know when enough is enough.'

'Should I take your plate?' asked Sarah, a little too eagerly.

'Please,' said Frank, 'but don't you throw any of that out.

Someone should finish it, sometime. Don't like seeing waste.'

'You want me to keep it for you? For tomorrow?' asked Sarah.

'No, no need, it would be unfair of me to lean any more on your hospitality. I should be making my way home to see my family.'

An uneasy silence fell as Ned and Sarah cast their eyes to the floor. Frank sensed a problem immediately.

He waited.

The silence continued.

'Is anyone going to tell me?' he asked.

'They're all gone, Frank,' said Sarah, lifting her head as she spoke.

Frank saw her glassy look and was confused. 'All gone where?'

When Ned spoke he tried not to make eye contact with Frank. 'They've all gone to the grave,' he said.

Frank was stunned. 'What? Not smallpox?'

'No. We've been lucky here, but the consumption has been bad, real bad,' said Sarah, quickly but quietly. 'Whole families have been taken, Frank.'

Frank's face showed his bewilderment. 'When?'

Ned looked at Sarah. 'Three years?'

'Close to four,' corrected Sarah softly.

'Both of my brothers?'

Sarah's voice was gentle. 'Albert went first, then Robert. Your mother, she nursed them to the last. But all were gone within one winter.'

With a touch of anger, Frank said, 'And no word was sent to me?'

'Your mother made us promise not to tell you,' continued Sarah. 'I said I could write. But she said there was nothing

44

you could do, and that it would only worry you into an early grave. She also said that you told her not to write.'

It was true, Frank had told his mother to forget about him and not make contact. This severance had been offered in the way of an apology, with him saying he did not deserve to be her son. However, he had tried to write on several occasions, but it was such a painful process and he had no idea what to say, so he just gave up. She in turn, had ignored his wishes and written on each of his birthdays for the first three years of the sentence, and when she stopped, he was sure it was because he had failed to reply. Now he sat, numbed to the bone, trying to absorb what he was being told.

'The property?' he finally asked.

'The bank foreclosed and boarded it up,' said Ned.

'I'll get it back,' said Frank. It was a rash boast as he didn't have a penny to his name.

'It's in bad repair. Some squatters got in a while back and lit a fire in the main room. The floor has a hole in it. Just rats live there now.'

'Which bank?'

'Agricultural, I guess. Nearly everyone uses the Agricultural Savings and Loan.' Ned looked over at Sarah for confirmation and she nodded in agreement.

'You still got my gun, Ned?'

Ned was hesitant. 'Yes,' he said slowly.

'You're not going to do anything hasty, are you, Frank?' asked Sarah.

Frank's fingers were drumming on the table. 'I'm thinking,' he said.

'About what?' asked Sarah. 'Holding up the bank?'

'I need money.' Frank's stopped drumming and clenched his fists.

'If we had any, we'd give it to you, Frank,' said Ned.

Frank looked at both of them in the flickering light of the oil lamp and his anger was suddenly swamped by a surge of stark reality. His eyes welled with tears. This homecoming, which he'd dreamed of for years, was now being dashed upon a rocky shore like some rudderless lifeboat in a heavy sea. He wondered if drowning might be a blessed relief. His family had gone without him and he felt alone, helpless and abandoned.

8

HOPEFULLY NOTHING

Down in Stilwell

Frank woke with a start and for a brief moment he thought he was still in prison. With relief he realized that he was free, only to then feel the chill of his situation as a penniless dependant. He squeezed his eyes shut and wondered if it would be better to be back in Cell Block E, where at least he knew the game and how it was played. Here it was different. He may have returned to Stilwell where he had grown up, but it was now an unfamiliar place and unsympathetic to any fond memories. It was a foreign world somewhere between disappointment and despair. Could hell be worse? He lay on the narrow cot, rigid, with legs stretched out as he fought the urge to pull the blankets over his head like a child seeking sanctuary from a fearful noise.

Ned tapped on the door and called his name softly.

Frank was jerked from his dismal thoughts and grunted a response. However, he didn't get up. He just lay there and listened to the muffled conversation in the kitchen and knew it was about him. But still, he didn't get up.

It was Sarah who entered the room nearly an hour later and quietly sat on the edge of the low crib, tapping him gently on the side of the upper leg to give her room to sit. He felt obliged to say something in way of a reason for his idleness, but couldn't think of what. Should I feign sickness as an excuse, he thought.

But it didn't come to that as she started to speak in a soft voice and started to tell a story, much like a mother reciting a bedtime tale to a child. She talked about the loss of her son Todd, and at first, Frank thought she was about to lay blame at his feet and accuse him of the young boy's death. But as he lay there and listened to Sarah, he realized that she was sharing a confidence for the first time. She was opening up her heart and telling of the grief she had felt on seeing the soaked and lifeless body of her son. She spoke of the place she had found herself after the funeral and that it was like being trapped in a deep well where the only light was not much more than a small dim circle high above.

'What did you do?' asked Frank in a whisper.

'I went to bed and refused to get up, like you are doing now.'

'For how long?'

'Several weeks. I refused to eat in the hope that I would starve to death.'

Frank swallowed hard before he said, 'I heard you were in mourning and had decided not to speak to anyone, but I didn't know about ...' He swallowed again. 'But you survived.'

'I did.'

Frank's mouth was dry as he asked, 'How?'

'I finally came to my senses and realized that I could not go back in time and change what had happened. And, that if I did die, that too would change nothing. I also saw that I was being weak, yet all my life I had prided myself on my strength. My father used to call me the strong one of the family. I knew that the content of my character was more than self-pity. I knew I could be depended upon. So I got up and went back to work.'

'What sort of work was that?' asked Frank.

'Washing, cleaning, cooking, fixing. I scrubbed this house from top to bottom. I emptied every cupboard, drawer and chest.'

'What did that do?'

'It forced out the feelings of my own misfortune and showed that I was still strong.'

'I have no work, no job, and no ...' Frank couldn't get the word out, but it was there at the forefront of his mind. He was a man with no special skills or trade. Sure, he could turn a hand to the odd job but not much more. His life had been one of taking whatever whenever the opportunity arose.

'There is much to be done,' said Sarah. 'Ned does his best and I appreciate his every effort, but he has lost his spark and just plods. If you were to pitch in, then it would help both you and me. Might even spark up Ned. He sees you as a big brother.'

'He's five years older than me.'

'Age has nothing to do with nothing. It's how you believe and behave that counts. I'm two years older than Ned, but my needs haven't changed and I haven't changed my ways or my hopes since I was fourteen.' Sarah patted his leg to get up then left as quietly as she had arrived, closing the door behind her.

Frank felt a sense of shame for his indulgence in believing that he was the only one to ever feel despair. She was right, he was being weak and that was not his true nature. He had always been the cocky one with the smart mouth who was willing to take a chance when others were unsure and shy. And he was the one who could cajole those around him to follow. He had the ideas and could formulate them into a plan and act them through. He was the one who could bring home the bacon. That's what his father said to him when he was just eight years old. Mind you, he had just stolen a hindquarter of pork from the butcher's cold room down on Floyd Street and carried it home tucked up under his jacket.

Breakfast was a cup of weak coffee and a thin mix of salted maize meal, while Sarah dropped the none too subtle hint that the house was in need of urgent repairs. Frank took the lead and with Ned, commenced to inspect the outside. A close look at the front porch and at the cladding on the weather side of the house showed that some serious work was required. Previous patching up had been done, but it was rough and only short term. When quizzed, Ned pointed out that there was no money for the necessary lumber to do the job.

'We'll have to use what we can find, then,' said Frank with a dash of authority.

'From where?' asked Ned. 'Everything around has been picked to the bone over the past ten years. It's been lean for everyone, everywhere.'

'What about my family's place?' asked Frank.

'Boarded up,' said Ned.

'So, we need boards, don't we?'

'But it belongs to the bank now, Frank.'

'Too bad,' said Frank with just a touch of spite.

They harnessed up the only remaining horse in the barn. She was an old big-footed girl named Rosie, who pulled an even older wagon that creaked and groaned with every turn of the wheels as they slowly plodded over to what was once Frank's family home. When the house came into view, in between the silver maples, Ned stopped and silently looked at Frank to gauge his reaction.

Frank just looked without saying a word, then eased himself down from the seat and walked over to the derelict building. In silence he circumnavigated the exterior in slow silence, touching a wall or a window sash every now and then with Ned just two or three steps behind.

It could not be denied that the property was indeed in a poor state of disrepair, just as Ned and Sarah had said. And while the bank had boarded up the doors and windows, and placed signs on all four sides advising that trespassers would be prosecuted, entry had occurred and damage done. The worst was in the main room where a fire had all but burnt the house down, leaving a large hole in the floor and smoke damage to the walls and the pressed tin ceiling. In the kitchen, Frank paused before the fireplace where the large cast iron stove had been removed, as had the copper kettle in the outhouse washroom.

'Sorry you had to see it like this, Frank.'

Frank just nodded and continued his inspection, noting where he could take the timber they needed. When he walked back out onto the front porch, he said, 'We'll lift all these boards and take off the cladding on the north side.'

'You sure, Frank?'

'Yeah, that will give us a full wagon.'

'No, I mean, it's your family home. You don't want to try and get it back and fix it up?'

Frank shook his head. 'No, what was here has all gone.'

'But the memories?'

'Best they go too, Ned. At least for the time being.' Frank patted Ned's shoulder. 'Time to get to work.'

'What about the bank? You saw the signs. They won't be happy.'

Frank's hand now squeezed Ned's bony shoulder as he said firmly, 'Ned, was I ever a man who gave a hoot about keeping the banks happy?'

'Well, no, but–' Ned's concern slowly turned to a weak smile as he looked at Frank. 'No, not that I can ever recall.'

'So, what's changed, then?'

Ned's smile broadened. 'Well, hopefully nothing.'

'Damn, right, Ned. Hopefully nothing.' But Frank didn't believe it for a minute. Things had changed, but as Sarah had said, you just have to get on with it.

9

THE NEIGHBOUR

Repairs in Stilwell

Sarah was right. Work, good hard physical work, does take the mind off what was and what might have been, to put it firmly back in the here and now. And it all seemed to happen with a natural ease as soon the shirtsleeves were rolled up above the elbows.

The hand tools stored at the back of Sarah's barn were adequate for the repairs, however, it had been years since they'd been oiled and used. The blades of the handsaws were rusty and also in need of sharpening, but the essentials were there: mallets, clamps, wedges, block planes, files and even a bag of wire nails. The work began on the exterior walls and was easy enough, providing for quick results. But when the boards were lifted off the front porch, it was revealed that the supporting joists and stumps would need to be replaced. This required a second trip back to Frank's family home for heavier and longer beams.

It was just as they were leaving, with the wagon piled high that Frank and Ned were accosted by a neighbour, but not one that Frank had met before. Ned called him Harold when trying to offer a greeting.

The neighbour didn't want any of it. 'What do you think you are doing?' The voice was a challenging screech that was trying to sound commanding.

Frank sat and watched from the wagon and thought that any conversation was pointless. It was clear as crystal exactly what they were doing so he had to stop himself from calling back, what do you think we are doing, you idiot? But he restrained himself, until formally introduced. However, Ned couldn't get a word in any which way as Harold continued his rant.

'This 'ouse has been foreclosed by the bank and trespassers will be prosecuted. It says so on the signs.'

Frank now became a little amused as he realized that 'Arold didn't or couldn't pronounce the letter H.

Finally, Harold drew breath, just long enough for Frank say, 'Let's go, Ned.'

'Who are you?' called Harold.

Ned answered back. 'This is Frank, Frank Nester. He's the last surviving son of the Nester family. Albert and Robert's younger brother.'

'Oh,' said Harold, 'the jailbird.'

Frank felt the heat rise in his veins, but he sat tight and just said again to Ned, 'Let's go.'

'You can't go thieving where and when you like, you know,' yelled Harold as the wagon creaked away at a snail's pace. 'I'm going to buy this land, and I don't want anything taken from it. What you're doing is thieving.'

Frank didn't give the incident with 'Arold Benson much thought other than to refer to Harold as an upstart idiot. But Sarah showed concern in her eyes when told. Ned said that it was best to be on good terms with the neighbours and that Harold was a man of means, who had acquired the property behind Frank's old home that went all the way down to the banks of Turtle Creek.

It was not till later in the week that it all got a bit serious, when Arthur McCutcheon turned up at Sarah's door seeking an explanation over the removal of lumber from the property. Frank knew Art, who was a young deputy in the Stilwell sheriff's office at the time of his trial, but it was just a passing acquaintance and there had never been any animosity between the two. In fact, Art's mother had been friendly with Frank's mother, so Art was seen to be a half decent young man, if also half an idiot for joining the law straight from school.

When Sarah came onto the porch to see what was going on, Art quickly removed his hat as a sign of good manners and respect.

Frank noticed this courtesy before he asked, 'Why is the sheriff's office worrying about this matter? I thought you'd have more important things to do than chasing up someone who took some old siding off their parents' house, so that a neighbour's home could be fixed.'

Art scuffed the ground with his boot. 'Frank, it's not your parents' house any more; it belongs to the bank, lock, stock and barrel. And you certainly can't go pulling it down, even if it is to repair Sarah's place.'

'Have you seen the state of it?' asked Frank, pointing down the valley to where the remains of his family home stood.

Art scuffed his boot into the dirt again. 'Yes, I've seen.'

'It's a knock-down, now.'

'Maybe, but that's for the bank to decide.'

'Why are you sticking up for the bank? As the law, you should stick up for people like Sarah.'

'He's just doing his job,' whispered Sarah.

'That's who I work for now, Frank. I'm with the Agricultural Savings and Loan Bank.'

'I thought you were a deputy.'

'Got laid off four years ago and I've got to work.'

'A bailiff, eh?'

Art nodded. 'That's right.'

'But your job's been done. The house doesn't have any tenants. Even the squatters have gone. So you don't have anyone to evict.'

'I don't only evict, Frank, I look after bank property that has been foreclosed.'

'And how did that happen?'

'The foreclosure?'

'Yeah.'

'Your brother Albert borrowed against the property.' Art gave a dejected shrug. 'Then he got sick and was unable to pay back the loan. But the bank only foreclosed after Robert and your mother had passed.'

'How much was owing?' asked Frank.

'I don't know exactly, Frank, I would have to ask the manager.'

'Well, what's done is done, but on this particular instance why not just turn a blind eye, Art, and put it down to squatter damage.'

Art noticed that Frank's tone had mellowed somewhat since his younger days, but as an employee of the bank there was no way for him to meet any such plea. It could cost him his job.

'I can't. I have a formal complaint from a person who is interested in buying the property. They put their grievance in writing.'

'Well, well, well,' said Frank, 'and I wonder who that could be.'

'I'm not obliged to say,' said Art.

'You don't have to,' said Frank. 'But let me fix this myself. You can go back and say that it's just a small neighbourly dispute and I'll go over and have a talk to our neighbour Mr 'Arold Benson.' Frank was not hiding his scorn as he spoke.

That's the old Frank I remember, thought Art. 'Can't let you do that, Frank. But if you put all the timber back then I can have a talk with the branch manager and smooth things over.'

'Put it back, did you say? Put it all back? Can't you see? It's all been used up. It's now fixed to this building.' Frank stamped his boot on the newly repaired decking on the porch to emphasize the point.

Ned stepped back as if to protect Sarah. He had seen this

all before, but not for the past twelve years. Frank was building up steam, which usually meant he was about to explode.

'Like hell I'm going to put it back,' he bellowed, 'because of some upstart idiot. And you shouldn't even be asking, Art. That place, where my parents and brothers lived, is close to falling down. It's been set on fire and the stove and kettle have been taken. Where were you then, to protect the property for your precious bank?'

'Now don't go getting upset, Frank. I'm just trying to do my job.'

Frank's tapping foot on the newly repaired porch timbers was beating like a drum, but somehow he got his rage back under control. 'This conversation is over,' he said. 'And you should leave, now.'

'I'm going,' said Art as he placed his hat back on his head, 'to let you cool down and think it over. If you do decide to put the lumber back, just stack it up beside the house, then I'll do my best to smooth everything over. Otherwise, Frank, it's not over. And I don't want to see you back inside.'

'That ain't going to happen, Art. I'm not going back inside for anyone. Not ever, never. You got that?'

'Well, I sure hope it doesn't come to that,' said Art as he pulled down on the brim as a farewell to Sarah before walking back over to his horse and thinking that this is precisely where it is going, right back down the road to the State Penitentiary in Lansing, Frank, if you are not careful.

10

THE RED BARN

Summons in Stilwell

In the end, Frank went peacefully. The young deputy, who arrived with Art, handed over a summons for Frank to appear before the clerk of the court to answer a charge of trespass and the unlawful removal of property. It had been Sarah's intervention that had soothed Frank to some sort of semi-calm, saying that it would harm his case for a resolution if he were to make a fuss. This was only after Frank's initial reaction was to kill Harold.

'Where's my gun?' he had shouted. 'I'll kill that idiot.'

'No need for that,' said Art, who had skilfully talked the bank's branch manager around to proceeding by means of a hearing, and to leave out the word theft on the paperwork. To do so would have resulted in Frank's arrest.

'Shooting Harold is not a sensible solution,' said Sarah quietly. 'Suitable, maybe, but sensible, no.'

Her sense of humour both surprised and quietened Frank, who said, 'Yeah, I know. But I'm not going back to prison for any man.'

'It's just a hearing, Frank,' said Art, 'not a trial. People are going before the clerk all the time on bank matters and nobody is being locked up. You took from what was once your home and that's no sin in these times of repossession. Besides, it's either go see the clerk or run away.'

'This is where you grew up,' said Sarah in support of Art. 'This is where you belong.'

When Frank thought about it, he agreed; she was right. 'Still, I feel like I'm in a trap,' he said.

Sarah leant in and said softly, 'We're all in a trap of some sort. That's just the way it is for folks like us.'

Frank pondered Sarah's remarks on the journey into Stilwell with Art and the deputy, and as depressing as it was, she was right. And when he took a good look at Art, he realized that even he was trapped in a kind of way, by working for a bank and foreclosing neighbours' property.

'Folks like us,' he mumbled to himself. 'Always the losers in life.'

The hearing, before the clerk of the court, who Frank didn't know, was brief and to the point when he finally got to the head of the queue. The long line was mostly full of loan defaulters who were being evicted from their homes, and the clerk was pushing them through like passengers buying railway tickets. His face was one of dispassionate tolerance for this most distasteful of jobs.

Another trapped man, thought Frank.

'You have thirty days to return any lumber removed from the property and make good to the satisfaction of the owner who is the Stilwell Branch of the Agricultural Savings and Loan Bank. Or, pay $110.35 in retribution.'

The retribution sum may have been $1,000 for all the chance that Frank had of raising such a sum of money over the next thirty days.

On leaving the courtroom, Ned resigned himself to the task at hand and suggested that they get on with undoing the work they had done on Sarah's house. However, Frank was in no such mood and said, 'Not straight away. I need to think first.'

A week later he was still thinking and still in a mood. Ned

told him that they had to just get on with it or they would dig themselves into a hole with the law.

This brief comment prompted Frank to ask, 'Ned, did you ever go looking for the money Todd buried up on Little Peak after I went to prison?'

Ned confirmed he had, but with no success. 'It's like looking for a lost pin. I even tried to think like young Todd, as if I was him, and where I would bury it. But that didn't help.'

Later that night Frank suggested quietly to Ned that they go and take a last look, just in case. Ned didn't protest. There was nothing to lose. So, early the following day they headed up to Little Peak on foot with shovels, only to return at sunset empty-handed and with blisters.

When Sarah quizzed them on what they had been doing, Frank came clean, but skirted around any involvement of Todd, just saying that someone else had buried the money on their behalf. But this ended up making Frank look foolish, as Ned had come clean with Sarah years ago out of a repentant conscience and a desire for forgiveness. Unfortunately for Frank he had failed to pass on any details of this contrite confession.

'Where would a fourteen-year-old boy bury such an amount?' she said. 'I must admit, it is a mystery, even to his mother. But wouldn't it come in handy if it could be found?'

Frank glared at Ned, not about to open his mouth and look more like an idiot than he felt, while Ned shifted his gaze to study with interest the frayed curtain fabric hanging from the front room windows.

The next day Sarah went with them and again the following day, yet regardless of this additional effort, they were no closer to finding the money. The only marks left from their concerted endeavours were the small shovelled holes, which added to the rabbit borrows that infested parts of Little Peak.

It was near sunset on the fourth day when Frank was ready to declare defeat that Sarah made comment on the sun shining off Brimley's barn. Dave Brimley's property was down on the west side of Little Peak where he had run dairy cattle for nearly thirty years.

'Lord, that's a fine barn,' she said. 'Just where does Dave Brimley get the money to paint his barn all fancy-like in hard times like these?'

Ned just shook his head and said, 'It does look good, though, doesn't it?'

At first Frank paid no attention as he continued to scrape at the earth. When he did finally look up, the sun, now low in the sky, lit up the side of the red barn as if it was on fire. It seemed to glow and for a moment it didn't look real, but more like a painting in bright magnificent colours of red, orange and gold. It was truly a vision to behold. And that's when the realization hit him.

'Ah, no,' he said. 'Not Brimley.'

Ned looked confused.

Sarah shaded her eyes as she kept looking at the vivid scene. 'I wonder why Dave chose red and not white?'

'Because he could afford to,' muttered Frank.

'What do you mean?' asked Ned.

'Have you ever seen a barn look that good, even in good times?'

'Well, no,' said Ned. 'I guess not.'

'And that's because you only do those sort of things when the money is no problem.'

'And when's that?' asked Ned.

'When you get an unexpected windfall, that's when.'

Sarah twigged to what Frank was on about. 'You think Dave Brimley may have found the money?'

'Well, why don't we go and ask,' said Frank as he shouldered his shovel and started walking towards the barn. Sarah and Ned looked at each other briefly, and followed.

The three caught Dave Brimley by surprise near the milking shed behind the barn. The expression on his face only heightened Frank's suspicions. However, Dave quickly composed himself and told Frank that he had heard that he was back in town.

What followed was a little strained country chitchat, before Dave said that he had to get on with the business of milking. Sarah commented to Dave on a story she had heard that he had a milking machine and could she see how it worked. Brimley coughed and spluttered maybe she could later, but not today, as he was far too busy.

Frank said, 'A milking machine, now that sounds expensive. Where could you possibly get the money for such a modern contrivance as a milking machine?'

'I work hard,' was Dave's defensive response.

'So does everybody else,' replied Frank drily, before saying, 'You know, Dave, the three of us have been chatting away next to your beautiful big red barn and each of us with a shovel in our hand, and not once have you even asked, what the hell have we been doing?'

Dave's eyes flashed side to side before he said, 'None of my business what you've been doing.'

'Why not?' asked Frank. 'Three neighbours from down Turtle Creek way, up here on Little Peak with shovels, and right next to your property and digging around like rabbits. For what?'

'I let others keep their business to themselves and I keep

my business to myself.'

'I bet you do, Dave. But maybe it's time you shared a little of that business with us. Like where and when you found the money?'

Dave paused a little too long before he said, 'What money?' And his voice was a touch shaky.

'The money that has allowed you to paint up your farm like a fire engine and buy a milking machine.'

'I don't know what you are talking about.'

'I think you do, Dave, and if I have to belt it out of you with my shovel, I'll do it.'

'You can't do that. I'll go to the sheriff.'

'And tell him what, Dave?' Frank drew the sound of Dave's name out to emphasize the foolishness of such a notion. 'He might ask you about stealing stolen money, especially after he has had a talk to me.'

'You won't tell him anything. It was you who stole it in the first place and I knew it was you all along. When I saw you and Ned digging around up here before you went to prison, I got a notion as to what you were doing. You were searching but I found what you were looking for, and what you find in this life, you get to keep.'

'Not necessarily,' said Frank who had turned his shovel around so that the blade was now upright in his hand.

'Maybe we can come to an agreement,' said Sarah. 'After all, Dave has found what has been lost, so he should receive a reward, that's only fair.'

Dave was nodding his head vigorously.

'Looks like he's already taken his reward in red paint,' said Frank.

'And a milking machine,' added Ned.

'How much is left?' asked Sarah.

Dave hesitated. 'Not a lot.'

'What do you mean, "not a lot"? There was $2,573.58,' said Frank.

'You sure?' asked Sarah with surprise.

'It's indelibly imprinted on my mind,' said Frank. 'That was the amount reported by the Mo-Pacific.'

'I couldn't believe it when I found it,' said Dave. 'Never seen so much. I said it was manna from heaven, but Olive said different. She knew where it had come from and she wanted to take it back, but I convinced her that if we spent it on the farm and not ourselves, then it would be all right. Things were tough and I knew they were going to get tougher. When it really got bad and we saw the panic of '93 and there was no money around, well, it was like a godsend. It saved our farm.'

'Saved it! It was your red letter day,' said Frank looking at the side of the red barn. 'When did you find it?'

'Eight years ago.'

'Where?'

'Sticking out of a rabbit hole up near the top corner fence. The rabbits had dug it up.'

'How much have you got left?'

'A few hundred, I guess.'

'A few hundred? Is that all?' Frank was incensed.

'It's better than nothing,' soothed Sarah.

'Where do you keep it?' Frank was now tapping an agitated foot.

'Out in the barn. I wanted to put it under our bed but Olive said it was not to be kept in the house. She said she didn't want to see it, ever.'

'Well, she's going to see it now. Go and get Olive so she knows what's going on,' said Frank.

There was silence and Dave didn't move.

Frank went to tell him again to go and fetch his wife, but Sarah interjected. 'Frank, Olive passed away last year.'

Frank immediately knew he'd put his foot in it and mumbled an apologetic, 'Oh, I didn't know. What happened?'

Dave didn't answer.

'Consumption,' said Sarah.

An empty silence hung like an icy chill in the air till Frank said, 'Get the money, Dave.'

They all walked to the large barn and down to the far end, where Dave opened one of the winterfeed boxes and removed some harnesses. He bent over, reaching down low and pulled out an old dirt stained mail sack. He tipped the contents onto the floor.

After counting, what remained of the stolen money was just $287.15.

'Is that it?' asked Frank.

'It will allow you to pay retribution to the bank, Frank,' said Sarah.

'And have some over,' said Ned.

Then Dave said, 'What about my share?'

'Your share? You've had your share,' said Frank.

'My milk doesn't cover my bills,' said Dave. 'I still need to put food on the table.'

'Yes, Frank, we should leave Dave with something,' said Sarah. 'To help him out.'

'Anyway,' said Dave. 'Why should I give you any of this? You've got all that money from the second heist you pulled up on Spring Hill.'

'Second heist? That wasn't me and Ned, you idiot,' said Frank.

'Who was it then?'

'How the hell do I know? If I knew, I'd go after them, wouldn't I, for being locked up for something I didn't do.'

'Don't believe you,' said Dave, but he seemed a little confused.

'You are an idiot. If I had taken all that money I'd be living the good life, wouldn't I? Just take a look at me. Do I look rich?'

Dave gave a brief glance at Frank's appearance. 'Maybe you buried that too and forgot where.'

'We didn't forget where we buried this,' said Frank, pointing at the money now stacked neatly on the floor. 'We just didn't know where it was buried.'

'How come?'

'Someone else buried it for us.'

'Who?'

'My son, Todd,' said Sarah.

'Oh,' said Dave. 'I didn't know.'

'He was with us and drowned in the creek, just after,' said Ned, 'before he could tell us where he hid it.'

'Young Todd was involved in the Spring Hill heist?'

'He was only involved in handling the horses and hiding the money,' said Frank. 'But he had a share of the takings coming his way.'

'How much?' asked Dave as he looked at Sarah.

'More than what's left here,' said Frank.

'Do you want to take it, Sarah?' asked Dave.

'Not all of it,' said Sarah. 'Frank, let Dave keep half.'

'Half!' Frank twitched with agitation.

'What then?' asked Sarah, her voice calm.

'He can keep one hundred dollars.'

'One fifty,' said Dave in response.

'That's more than half, Dave, you idiot. If I'm not happy with giving you half, why would I then agree to give you more than half?'

'Dave?' asked Sarah, trying get a response.

'One twenty five,' said Dave.

'Frank, let Dave keep $125.'

Frank was ready for an argument but when he saw the look in Sarah's eyes he relented and nodded his head slowly in reluctant submission.

Sarah nodded back. 'It will give you $162.15, Frank. And at the moment you need that money.'

Frank did the arithmetic but not as fast, and she was right on the amount. And yes, he needed the money because he had none. He was stony-broke and living off the backs of Sarah and Ned. However, any virtue that may have come from the decision to share what was left with Dave Brimley was lost on Frank. He sulked all the way back from Little Peak, saying nothing to Sarah or Ned as he strode ahead mumbling, 'Another trap, that's what it was, just another trap in a life full of traps.'

11

AN UNLOADED GUN

Cooking up in Stilwell

The following morning, as Frank lay in bed listening to Sarah cooking in the kitchen, he mulled over the events of the past day. His conclusion was that he had been cheated out of what was rightfully his and kept thinking of what could have been had Todd not died. With his share of the money it would have meant good times, he told himself, of wine, women and song – or at least, whiskey, dancing girls and saloon music. He wouldn't have stayed in Stilwell, he told himself, but left for Kansas City in a search for adventure and therefore not been implicated in the second heist. These jumbled thoughts made him sore over his lot in life, but they were just an immature indulgence, a fantasy mixed with idiot notions that fate had mistreated him with her ill will. I deserved better, he concluded, while not once considering if had ever done anything wrong in his life.

When Sarah called for him to arise, he rolled onto the edge of the cot and searched for a lost left boot. It was under the bed and when he reached to find it, his eyes fell upon the neatly carved letters, FN, NW and TL on the timber frame of the bed. He looked closer and saw that just below it, also carved with a neat hand, was 1885. He sat back up and pulled on the boot while repeating the letters in his mind.

It was when Sarah called out, 'Ned Wilson and Frank Nester, you better come now, your breakfast is ready,' that he understood what the letters meant. FN – Frank Nester, NW – Ned Wilson, and TL – Todd Lennon, and 1885 was the year that the three of them had pulled off the mail van raid.

Frank looked around to realize that this was Todd's room. He had been blind to the signs of that time, which still remained all these years on. The shelf above the bed held a framed ink drawing of Chief Sitting Bull taken from an illustrated magazine. At the other end was a small carved horse with a rider, and next to it was a green spinning top with the neatly coiled whipcord looking like a miniature lariat.

Frank felt his stomach roll from the guilt of his early morning thoughts of being hard done by. He had been telling lies. The worst kind of lies; the ones you tell to yourself and believe. Had he said no to Todd, back when Ned introduced him to the 14-year-old boy with the horsemanship skills to be their third man on the forthcoming mail van raid, then Todd would still be alive, and that was the truth. He would now be twenty-eight years of age and older than Frank had been back in 1885. Frank rubbed his thumb across the carved initials and the date as he said aloud, 'You're an idiot, Frank Nester and you need to grow up.'

'We can replenish the pantry,' said Sarah on greeting Ned and Frank to the kitchen table, 'when we go into Stilwell to pay the bank.'

'You could cook pie,' said Ned, adding to her enthusiasm.

Frank remained deep in thought and said nothing.

'You don't like pie?' said Sarah to Frank.

As if jolted from a sleep, Frank said, 'No, I mean, yes. Pie, that would make a fine feast.'

Sarah bent forward a little. 'You still feeling annoyed about Dave and the money, Frank?'

Frank looked up at Sarah. 'No, not any more. I have blessings that I have yet to count.'

Ned caught Sarah's eye and raised an eyebrow, while in return Sarah just nodded before saying, 'Yes, we all have.' She then dried her hands on her apron and announced, 'Before we leave for Stilwell, we need to visit Harold first.'

Frank wondered, for what possible reason?

'And, Frank,' she said with authority, 'will you please bring your gun?'

'Do you want Frank to shoot Harold?' asked Ned.

'Hopefully, not. Provided he cooperates.'

'What do we do when we get there?' asked Ned.

'Leave that to me.'

Ned squirmed in his seat. 'Is there any need for me to come along, then?'

'Yes, I want you both there.'

Ned scratched at his ear. 'And do what?'

'Provide me with any assistance should it be necessary.'

'What sort of assistance?' asked Frank.

'I'm not sure at the moment.'

Ned looked over at Frank and shrugged.

Frank just nodded towards Sarah without argument and said, 'Sure. Ned has my gun somewhere, and hopefully it still works.'

When Ned handed Frank his handgun, which had been stored in a large chest in Sarah and Ned's bedroom, it brought back instant memories. He had won it in a card game over in Olathe in Johnson Country on the day of his twentieth birthday. Then the Smith & Wesson Number 3 was almost brand new while the cavalry holster that it came in dated back to Civil War days. The story went that the holster had belonged to one of Captain William Quantrill's men who had participated in the Lawrence Massacre. True or not, Frank didn't know, but he did wonder if the owner could have been either Frank or Jesse James, which would have added both notoriety and value to his winnings.

When he asked Ned for the ammunition to load his revolver, Sarah said that it would not be needed. But she did say that Frank should display to all that he was carrying a gun. On any other occasion Frank would have refused to carry an empty gun as it made no sense, but something told him to go along with the ruse, whatever it may be.

The ride over to Harold's property was slow and silent of

words, just the accompaniment of the creak and groan of the old wagon. On arrival it was apparent from just a quick glance by Frank that 'Arold was indeed a man of means. Sarah directed Ned to pull the wagon up to the front door and called to the maid, who had come out on to the wide portico, to tell Mr Benson that he had company. When Benson arrived at a brisk walk from around the side of the house, with sleeves rolled up, he immediately showed that he was not in a disposition to welcome anyone.

His response was cold and abrupt. 'I don't want any trouble,' he said.

'Trouble? Why would there be trouble?' asked Sarah with a soothing tone. 'We are just on our way to the Stilwell courthouse to resolve the concerns that you raised with the Agricultural Savings and Loan Bank.'

'So you've made good the repairs?'

'No, not at this stage, but rest assured, this matter will be settled before the day is done.'

'That makes no sense,' said Harold. 'But I'll take you at your word.'

Frank could not make out for the life of him where any of this was going and just wanted to leave. Benson was one of those men that by his very presence was as annoying as hell.

'You truly have a wonderful property,' said an admiring Sarah. 'It is a credit to you.'

Harold's demeanour changed with the flattery. 'It's taken a lot of work, but yes, it is looking fine.'

'Would you mind showing me around?'

Harold's manner changed back in an instant. 'I don't have the time.'

'Even after I have driven over here especially, as a sign of respect and good neighbourly manners to tell you that a—' Sarah paused. '—that a difficulty between us is to be resolved. I had hoped that you would wish to return such a gesture.'

Harold Benson's manner shifted again, as did his weight from foot to foot.

'Just a quick look,' said Sarah. 'No more than five minutes, and just me. Frank and Ned will wait on the wagon.'

'Very well,' conceded Harold.

Ned helped Sarah alight then got back up on the wagon to sit next to Frank. They both watched as Sarah, led by Harold, walked up the front steps and into his fine gleaming white house.

Just minutes later, Sarah arrived back at the door smiling and ready to bid farewell. Harold was more than ready for their departure as he turned and sought to take his leave.

'Don't be in such a hurry, Harold,' said Sarah before calling, 'Frank would now like to see the kitchen.'

Frank was about to advise that no, he didn't, but Harold beat him to it.

'Well, he can't.'

'Oh, yes he can,' said Sarah with an edge to her voice. 'You see, Frank is wearing a gun, and Harold, you're not. And Frank has just come out of jail for pleading guilty to a train robbery in which a man was killed with just one shot. Some say murdered. Frank could get down off that wagon and go anywhere he liked on your property, and you wouldn't be able to stop him.'

Harold's eyes narrowed. 'What's your case in point, Sarah, apart from threating me with harm by a convicted criminal?'

Frank was wondering the same thing and shifted his pistol from his hip towards his lap. This movement was made for no other reason than to seek comfort, as it had been a long, long time since he had worn a gun and it felt heavy and awkward. However, when Harold saw the adjustment he interpreted it to be a sign of intent to intimidate and took a step back.

'My case in point,' said Sarah, 'is that you can't stop Frank from taking a look in your kitchen.'

'But the sheriff can,' said Harold with a flash of defiance.

'But the sheriff is not here.'

Frank mumbled to Ned under his breath, 'What's going on?'

Ned was none the wiser, judging from the stunned look on his face.

'Frank,' called Sarah. 'You would like to see in the kitchen, wouldn't you? After all, that is where your mother's stove from her house now sits in pride of place. And I wouldn't be surprised if her copper kettle is now gracing the washhouse.'

It took a second or two for the impact of Sarah's announcement to sink in, but no more. Frank leapt off the wagon and strode into the house and out to the kitchen at the back. And there it was, the old family stove. However, now it had been cleaned up and refitted as a centrepiece in a new large kitchen.

Harold had followed and was saying, 'I can explain, and I am going to pay for it.'

Sarah, who was close behind, said, 'Good. We are going to Stilwell now, so let us save you a trip. If you give me the money, I will pay the Agricultural Savings and Loan Bank on your behalf, who is now the rightful owner of this fine stove and no doubt the fine kettle in the washhouse.'

Harold looked like a trapped animal that now conceded to his fate. 'I don't know how much I should pay,' he said.

'I do,' said Sarah. '$110.35.'

Frank had always considered himself to be a man with a flair for thinking through a plan and implementing it with precision. But, as he watched Harold count out the exact amount of money required to pay the court-directed costs and free him of any encumbrance to the bank, he could only marvel at her cleverness. She had, with guile alone, turned a defeat into a most unlikely victory, while he had played no more of a part than a piece of furniture upon a stage – and onc with an unloaded gun.

12

THE LIST

Writing it down in Stilwell

There wasn't just one pie, there were two. The beef pie was the largest and made from chunks of marbled meat cut from the hindquarter, which Ned ground for Sarah, using her long handled grinder. The recipe called for small brown onions, finely chopped carrots and freshly shelled peas. The mix was then pan fried before being spooned into the deep pastry base of the pan, smothered in a sea of dark brown gravy and sealed with a baking crust.

When served, each slice of pie was accompanied by a large spoonful of mashed potatoes, sprinkled with sea salt and dabbed with a dollop of butter. The other pie was baked with sugar on the pastry. It was a rich, sour cream lemon pie, and a second slice was impossible to refuse. When Frank finally pushed his empty plate away and looked down at his stomach, he was sure that a button on his shirt would pop. He couldn't remember when he had feasted so well and felt so full and content.

The praise that followed from Ned and Frank sprouted like blossoms in a spring garden, while Sarah quietly smiled as if such bounty was an everyday occurrence. But it wasn't. She had not been able to cook with ingredients like these in years. To now have bags of flour, baking powder, sea salt and granulated sugar in the pantry was a dream. And tomorrow there would be more of the joy of baking.

It was the following evening while Frank was sitting on the porch admiring the job he had done earlier that day whitewashing the railings, that Sarah engaged him in a conversation about his past. At first, he thought it was just curiosity on what it was like inside a penitentiary. However, she quickly turned her questions to his trial.

'Do you think about it much?' she asked.

'I used to, every day, when I was first inside but it did no good. It just eats away. I had to learn to accept what's done is done,' he replied.

'But why should it be done? You were found guilty of a crime you didn't commit.'

Frank gave a *so what* shrug. 'I pleaded guilty, so everybody thinks I'm guilty.'

'I don't.'

Frank leant forward and flicked a stuck dead bug off the dry whitewash. 'That makes two of us.'

'Three, with Ned,' said Sarah.

Frank gave a sly grin. 'Anyway, how do you know I didn't do it?'

'I know. Ned told me, and I trust Ned.'

'Yeah,' said Frank in agreement. 'I know of nobody else I trust more, and besides, I couldn't have done it without Ned.' He then hesitated, drew in a short breath, and said quietly, 'Or Todd. We were a team.'

Sarah tapped a finger against her chin in contemplation and the silence was agony for Frank before she said, 'So you would need someone like Todd as well?'

Frank coughed out a muffled yes, before he said, 'But you never pull the same stunt twice. Only an idiot would do that.'

'So it makes no sense to you, that second heist?'

'Well, not for us to do it,' said Frank, shaking his head slowly. 'But still, all that money. I thought our job was a big deal, but it was nothing to that second heist. And they got away with it.'

'So who were they?'

Frank felt his head involuntarily jerk a little. It was a clear and straightforward question, but one he had given up on ever knowing the answer long ago. It had become the unsolvable mystery, no matter which way he looked at it. Yet, coming from Sarah all these years later it somehow seemed to demand an answer. Just who did it?

'I don't know,' he said lamely. 'I guess it was someone from other parts and a lot smarter than me.'

'No, not someone,' said Sarah, 'but some others, at least three.'

Frank thought about it for a little. 'Yeah, you would need at least three.'

Sarah continued to tap her chin. 'But why did the mail clerk say it was just you, when it wasn't?'

'Davidson worked for the railroad and Dodd was after me. Dodd used to boast that he would get me. So I always took it that Dodd just paid Davidson off to say it was me.'

'Could Davidson be bought that easily?' asked Sarah.

Frank was starting to feel a little uneasy with this inquisition, not just because he had no idea where it was going, but because he had never asked himself these same questions with such clarity.

'Maybe, if Davidson was at fault for something,' replied Frank slowly, 'and that by saying it was me would have got him off the hook.'

'What do you mean?'

'Well, if he left the van unlocked, or was duped into opening up, when he should have kept the doors locked and the grills on the vents closed.'

'Did Dodd want to get you that bad that he'd threaten another employee?'

Frank nodded. 'He wanted me bad, all right. He knew I'd done the first heist and he wasn't going to let a second opportunity go by.' Frank continued to nod as if to convince himself that his explanation was right. 'And it made him look like a smart railroad detective, solving the crime so quickly. Truth is, he was too dumb and too lazy to find out who it really was.'

'Unless he was part of it?' said Sarah.

Sarah's words seemed to physically slap Frank with their simplicity. His head jerked back before asking, 'You've given this some thought, haven't you? And well before now?'

'I have tried to. Early on, Ned wanted to talk about it, so I listened. But I don't have any answers, just questions.'

When Sarah left to go back inside, Frank remained on the porch with his mind racing back through the questions she had raised. When he could find no new answers, his attention shifted to the realization of just how smart she was in noticing things and looking at them in such a curious way. It was not just Dave Brimley's red barn, but also the personal situation of Dave as a widower with no children, who was now left on his own to run a dairy farm. He dwelled for a moment on the amount of the stolen money and remembered Fletcher Prowse telling him just how heavy it would weigh in a mail sack. And he wondered what $100,000 would look like, all laid out on a barn floor. It seemed too great a sum to even contemplate.

'A mystery,' he mumbled to himself. But deep down inside he knew there was an answer for everything in this world. The trick, however, was knowing where to look, just like up on Little Peak. You had to do what Sarah did, look around and see what is out of place and ask the obvious question – why?

When Sarah handed Frank a page of notepaper, the following evening after dinner, he wasn't sure what it was he was looking at. A first glance had him thinking it was some sort of a game with its list of people, not by name, but position. It read, starting from the top: *mail van clerk, railroad policeman, prosecutor, attorney, judge, jury.* And it was only when he got to the very end of the list and read the words *dead man*, and the name *Don DeLuca* that he twigged to the purpose of Sarah's list.

'You want names?' he asked.

'And where they now live,' she replied.

'You think we need to know where they are now?'

'If we want to find out who took the money, we do.'

'You think they will know?'

'No, not all, but some.'

'But I don't see how any of these folk would know. The judge and the prosecutor thought it was me. I even thought my attorney thought it was me, until he said he didn't. The mail clerk said it was me, but he was lying. Dodd didn't care if it was me or not. He was just after blood.'

'But you're just guessing,' said Sarah as she poked a finger at the notepaper that was still in Frank's hand. 'We need to ask certain people on this list what they knew; what they didn't know; and why they said the things they said.'

'I see,' said Frank, when actually he was still having a little difficulty in comprehending where this was going so he gave a grin. 'You know, when you handed me this list, I thought it might be part of a parlour game.'

The look on Sarah's face made it clear that she did not see this as a game at all. To her this was a serious matter. Frank realized that he had said the wrong thing and conceded that even out of courtesy, he should go along with it all, even though his instincts told him that it would come to naught. It was, however, not lost on him, this endeavour being made by Sarah. In fact, it was most touching that she would make such an effort. It was as if she believed in him, and he couldn't remember when anyone had held such a belief, other than his mother.

13

LOADED

The Stilwell recipe book

Little by little and bit by bit, over the following weeks, each name and snippet of possible whereabouts was transcribed into the back of a larger lined book that was kept in the kitchen and used for recipes, shopping lists and homemaking hints. It was a slow and fragmented process, but at no time did Sarah's diligence or enthusiasm wane. She treated this task of gathering and sorting much the same way she approached cooking, in an orderly and methodical manner amongst the clutter of pans and utensils upon the kitchen bench and sink. Intuitively, she knew when to shift a pot before it boiled over or lift a pan before it smoked. And likewise, in amongst her countless daily chores, she always had time to stop and record a new scrap of information when it came to mind, then quickly return to the task at hand.

Through some casual questions, after commenting on the weather, an old rail hand told Sarah down at the siding that he thought that Special Agent Rodney D. Dodd was still working for the Missouri Pacific Railroad up in Kansas City. However, the station agent, who had come down from the Kansas City depot less than two years before, couldn't recall any of the railroad police he knew as being called Dodd. Sarah noted in her book that a follow-up was required with a possible trip to Kansas City.

She visited Art McCutcheon at the bank on the pretence of thanking him again, for smoothing the way with the bank manager over Frank's transgression on removing lumber from bank property. He was only too happy to receive any appreciation as his job as bailiff brought little joy. And just as she was about to leave, she asked if he knew where Judge Chester Millbrook was now residing. He said he didn't, but would ask. Two days later, when she was at the co-operative store and saw Art by chance, she asked if he had found out anything. He said, apologetically, that it had slipped his mind but would chase up the answer. Niecey Armitage who was buying lamp oil at the time, overheard Art and Sarah's conversation and said that she had heard that the judge had passed away the previous year and was buried at Fort Smith.

Sarah quizzed Niecey on how she knew. She said her cousin, Jolly Armitage, who now lived in Fort Smith, had told her. Sarah wasn't too sure if she should trust this advice, as Niecey's nickname was Nicely, due to her tendency to tell people whatever she thought would please them. Sarah's bias against the Armitage clan was exposed when Art heard her say aloud to herself, 'Can you really rely on a family that give their children such silly names as Jolly and Niecey?' But, regardless, the information went into the book, along with a question mark and the note that the death of the judge may need to be confirmed.

Richard Jenkins, the prosecutor in Frank's second trial, was known to have embarked on a political career. He had tried getting endorsement with the Democrats. However, that proved to be difficult as their list of would-be candidates was long, so he worked for the party as a legal advisor in order to gain favour. It was not until 1895 that he was able to try for the US Senate, only to have his aspirations dashed when defeated by the Republican Lucien Baker. The ever resourceful and ambitious lawyer shifted his political aspirations to the Kansas State Senate and successfully won the seat of Topeka, which, like the rest of Kansas and the country at large, was doing its best to weather the economic depression that had clouded much of the 1890s.

Jenkins had campaigned on the declaration that he would represent the best interests of each and every Topekan citizen. To do so, would of course, require not just a massive effort but also the talent of a circus juggler. Since taking office, it was a common comment in local saloon gossip that little had been seen or heard of him. Maybe he was still practising his conjuring skills, noted Sarah in her book. She also assigned to him the status of a low priority to their investigations, as she really couldn't see what significance he might have on anything in particular. However, he was still alive, of sorts, and she knew they could find him at the State Capital if needed. When Frank read her note, he mentioned in passing that Jenkins was working for Missouri Pacific at the time he was the prosecutor. Sarah had assumed that he had just been hired by the railroad, not that he actually worked for them in a permanent capacity. She thought this situation to be somewhat curious. Frank couldn't see the significance, but Sarah raised Jenkins's priority from low to medium with a stroke of her sharpened pencil.

What had happened to Frank's defence attorney, Fletcher Prowse, was uncovered by Sarah when visiting the clerk of the Stilwell court to confirm the passing of Judge Millbrook. This was the same clerk who had set the conditions for remuneration to the bank for the lumber taken by Frank and Ned. Sarah expected to be recognized, as she had been at the court when retribution was paid. However, he seemed unaware of this fact when she stopped him on the steps of the courthouse.

'You may remember me,' she said. 'Sarah Lennon, and I will only take a moment of your time. Could you tell me if Judge Chester Millbrook is still alive?'

'No, sorry, I can't recall you, Mrs Lennon. As for the judge, he passed recently.' The clerk turned to leave.

'Just one other. Attorney Fletcher Prowse. Do you know where I could find him?'

'He is also deceased.'

Disappointment showed on Sarah's face before asking,

'Did you know him?'

'I met the judge, but not Attorney Prowse,' said the clerk. 'I only know of him by reputation.'

Sarah sensed that the clerk had an opinion on that reputation and was willing to voice it. 'Was he held in esteem?' she asked.

'Depends,' sniffed the clerk. 'Some say he was a brilliant advocate. Others are not so sure.'

'What do you say?' asked Sarah.

'I have no idea, but temperance and the law go hand in hand.'

Sarah got the message. 'Just when did he pass?' she asked.

'Four or five years ago in Topeka. I believe he was working right up to the hour of his death.'

'Does he have family?'

The clerk pulled his watch from his waistcoat and checked the time. 'I know that he has a daughter. I met her when she made an application for court papers of all the cases her father had defended. She was compiling a book on his life and times.' The clerk turned to go.

'Just one last question.' Sarah reached for his arm, but the clerk was now three steps away. 'Does she live in Topeka also?'

'Yes, on Quincy Street,' he said and tipped his hat as he said, 'Madam.' But it was said as an end to their exchange, not a friendly farewell.

Sarah called, 'Thank you for your time.' But she was just addressing the back of a dark suit as the clerk strode away.

The note in the recipe book that evening listed the daughter of Attorney Prowse as a high priority. Frank asked why.

'Because she may know the details of your trial.'

Frank responded by saying, 'But I already know those.'

To which Sarah replied, 'Do you?'

'Of course I do, I was there.'

'So when you told me that Attorney Prowse spoke to Judge Millbrook regarding your guilty plead, you were there?'

'Well, no, not then, but he told me about it.' Frank thought for a moment then said. 'Sort of.'

It was later that night that Frank conceded that maybe he didn't know as much about his trial as he thought. This caused him to seriously re-examine the mechanics of that second robbery, which led him back to the one person who knew exactly what had occurred – Davidson. The man Frank had dismissed as an idiot.

When Sarah casually asked Frank the following day what exactly Samuel Davidson had said as the witness for the prosecution, Frank found himself searching for the specifics. Finally, he said. 'He was acting, as if he was on a stage.'

'Was his story challenged by Attorney Prowse?' she asked.

'He hadn't arrived,' said Frank. 'He was late and Davidson had made his statement and left.'

'That is a travesty of justice,' said Sarah. 'He should have been questioned in detail to ensure that he was telling the truth or the jury would have taken his word against yours.'

'It didn't matter in the end,' said Frank. 'I pleaded guilty and the jury was stood down.'

Sarah mulled over the notes in the recipe book before asking, 'Do you think that Davidson was really there when the van was robbed?'

Frank went to say of course, after all, he was working for the Missouri Pacific Railroad and they said he was in the van. But he stopped and asked Sarah to repeat the question. When she did, he replied by simply saying, 'I don't know.'

It was Frank who visited the station agent and asked if he knew of a Mr Samuel Davidson. Frank returned and told Sarah that the agent had called Davidson the 'unlucky lucky man'. It seemed that after receiving a windfall from a sickly maiden aunt who had suddenly passed away and left him with an unexpected and generous sum of money, he had lost the lot.

Sarah responded with keen interest and a finger perched on the end of her chin before asking, 'When?'

'Think he said ten years ago, or so,' said Frank.

'Where is he now?' Sarah was once again the inquisitor.

'Well, he resigned from the railroad, and this is the unlucky bit. He invested most of his inheritance in railroad stock, which went belly up with the panic and is now living in poor circumstances at Lee's Summit. He went there to find work. The agent says he now does some odd jobs for the railroad.'

'We need to go and see him.'

Frank agreed without thought, but then added, 'And ask him what, precisely?'

'Precisely what happened in the van and why he believed it was you.'

'Will he tell us?' asked Frank.

'I think so, if you take along your gun.'

'Right,' said Frank before he added, 'Why?'

'Because this time it will be loaded,' said Sarah, 'and that may help Mr Davidson to remember.'

'Right,' said Frank. 'Loaded, this time.'

14

A LITTLE CRAZY

Misunderstandings in Stilwell

'Where do you suppose all that money went?' Sarah lifted the pencil from the page of the recipe book and touched the blunt end against her lips in contemplation.

Ned shrugged, while Frank thought out loud, 'Maybe south.'

'Why south?' quizzed Sarah.

'Just guessing because it hasn't turned up in Kansas.'

Sarah was now tapping the end of the pencil against her cheek. 'It couldn't just disappear. Money just doesn't disappear. It has to go somewhere.'

'Are you sure of that? It seems to disappear when I spend it,' said Frank.

'How do you spend that much?' contemplated Sarah. 'And if you had all that money, what would you spend it on?'

Ned went to respond, but Frank beat him to the punch. 'Buy a property, get some horses, maybe travel a little and never worry about being cold or hungry.' Frank looked at Sarah. 'What about you?'

Sarah raised her eyes to the ceiling as if looking for the answer and repeated the question. 'If I had all the money I wanted, and then some?'

'Yes,' urged Frank, waiting.

'I would buy a piano,' said Sarah with consideration.

'A piano, is that all?' It was said to show disappointment in her grand desire.

But Sarah hadn't finished. She stopped examining the ceiling and said, 'And a parlour to put it in. A big one, attached to a brand new house.'

Sarah's answer tickled Frank so much that he couldn't stop cackling, while saying, 'A piano, a parlour, and a new house,' Then he said, 'I didn't know you could play the piano.'

'I can't, but I would learn.'

'And what would you do then?'

'Give recitals.'

'Who to?'

Ned watched this banter going back and forward between Sarah and Frank with close interest.

'The Kennedys, the Ballards and the Boettichers. Oh, how I would love to show up the Boettichers with some fancy piano playing in my fancy new parlour.'

'The Boettichers don't live here any more, do they?' said Frank. 'Didn't they move to Paola a real long time ago?'

'Fifteen years ago, but I'd go and get them from Paola,' said Sarah with a smile. 'Just to show them that I had made good.'

'I didn't think you were that kind of person, Sarah Lennon,' said Frank.

'And what kind would that be? The show off kind?'

Frank nodded. 'Maybe I just don't know you well enough.'

'Frank, it's not only me that you don't know well enough. You don't know women at all and it's probably time you got some schooling.'

'From where?'

'Does it matter where? As long as it is from a woman.'

'What are you suggesting, a mail order bride?'

'No, that would be foolish. It is only with proper courting that your head will finally speak louder than your heart.'

'What is proper courting?'

'Where you really get to know someone and decide if you can trust them, especially with money.'

Frank was feeling a little uneasy with the conversation. Marriage was not for him.

'I know one thing,' he said. 'I need you to teach me how you cook.'

'Now why would you want me to teach you to cook?'

'So that I can learn how you think.'

'Think? What's cooking got to do with me thinking?'

'You think like you cook, with everything going on at once, but kind of still knowing what should be done next and when.'

'Not "kind of" at all. I do know what needs to be done and when. You'll never see a pot boil over on my stove.'

'No, I haven't, and that's what I mean. It seems to be really messy when you are doing it, but then everything comes together and works out fine.' Frank quickly added, 'Perfect every time,' to smooth out any unintended criticism of being untidy in the process.

Sarah pulled on some strands of hair that had fallen from a clip to tickle her ear. 'I have no idea where you get such notions, Frank Nester,' she said with a smile as she twisted and tugged at the locks.

The following morning, Ned was gone.

When Sarah read the note that he had left, she called him a silly fool.

Frank thought Ned was just outside getting wood.

'Why? What's he gone and done?'

Sarah bit at her bottom lip. 'He thinks that I have fallen for you and that I don't love him any more.'

Sarah handed Frank the note, which he took reluctantly

and read in silence then handed it back.

'Men can be such fools when it comes to women and for thinking such things,' she said with scorn.

Frank wasn't so sure, as he had interpreted the scribbled note differently to Sarah.

'Maybe,' he said but didn't believe it and asked for the note back so he could read it again.

It was a short goodbye. Ned said it was for the better and that they should be left to each other. To Frank it seemed that Ned had come to the conclusion that it was not just Sarah falling for him, but he for Sarah. Or not to put too fine a point on it, that they were responding to each other in kind.

'Why did you let me stay with you and Ned?' Frank asked.

'Because you are Ned's friend. His best friend. Better than family. He has always told me that.'

'Well, we both might need to remind Ned that I am only here because you were responding to his endorsement when I bring him home.'

'I'll go with you,' said Sarah.

'No, if I am going to catch him I will have to move quick, and I need to explain myself, on my own.'

'Do you know where he's gone?' Sarah was fidgeting and getting agitated.

'Unless you know better, I'd say that he's going to jump the morning freight up to the junction. If I leave now and hurry, I should make it. If I don't then I'm only guessing where he would go from there.'

Sarah couldn't make eye contact with Frank. 'He's being a fool.'

'Maybe, but I do know that I've been an idiot. I should have seen this happening. I should have been more respect-ful. Ned is the only family I've got.'

Sarah looked up and she was on the verge of tears. 'And me,' she said while continuing to bite at her bottom lip.

Frank bolted with no more than he had on and was just crossing the river at the ford, but still on the other side of the old corn patch, when he heard the freight whistle blow. When it came into view he was more than 300 yards away and had to sprint flat out to make it. Even then he only just managed to get a one handed grip upon the ladder of the second last boxcar.

With lungs burning he pulled himself up and hooked his arm through a rung and cursed.

'You better be on this train, Ned.'

He had seen two men jump off and three climb on about five cars up, but he was unable to identify if Ned was amongst the prohibited passengers.

The train quickly came to speed and was swaying and rattling along by the time he had climbed onto the roof. When he finally lowered himself over the edge and swung into the empty car, he was still out of breath and a little shaken. Age was catching up. What he could do in his head no longer translated into effortless strength and agility. Had he lost his precarious grip on the edge of the roof, he could have easily fallen from the boxcar. The consequences of such a plunge caused him to consider caution in future.

At Shawnee, where the train slowed to a walk, he was joined by an old timer that he helped on board by taking his bindle.

'No bedroll yourself? You travelling rough?' asked the old man.

'No,' said Frank, 'just out for the day chasing someone who I hope is in a boxcar further up.'

'Owe you money?'

'No, I owe him.'

'Never heard of that before,' said the senior brother, 'someone chasing to pay a debt.'

'No, me neither until today.'

As the train came into to the Kansas City rail junction it slowed. Frank waited till it was close to walking pace then carefully eased himself down from the boxcar. Once he got his footing, he ran forward to where he'd seen the three men climb aboard at Stilwell, only to find that all the cars were empty. He guessed that they had alighted from the other side of the train and with frustration, he had to wait for all the cars to pass before he could cross the tracks and search. But there was no sign of anyone.

With anxious stilted steps, he jogged across the field of tracks and crawled between shunting rolling stock. He even took the risk of climbing atop a wagon, to expose himself to the yard workers in order to get a better view.

But with no sign and the best part of an hour gone, Frank decided to walk over to where he and Ned had sat and talked before jumping a freight south after he'd come out of prison. Ned had said it was a good spot to stay out of the way of the authorities, while observing the locomotives as they hitched up to the rolling stock. He sat down, cursing himself for being such an idiot. Then, just as the nagging doubt of ever finding his friend was turning to a cold reality, he saw the familiar lean frame ambling across to the northern line. Frank stood and cupped his hands as he yelled. Ned looked back but didn't respond. Frank called again.

'Ned, wait, it's me, Frank,' and began to run after the loitering figure.

Ned showed surprise when Frank caught him up, but he remained silent.

'Where are you going?' asked Frank, not knowing what else to say.

Ned shrugged.

'We need to speak.' Frank was a little out of breath.

'About what?' Ned said reluctantly.

'You and me.'

'And Sarah?'

Frank was still trying to catch his breath. 'Yes, Sarah, too, but I need to do some explaining first.'

'No need, I've got eyes, I can see.'

'Well, you've seen all wrong. I don't want to come between you and Sarah.'

Ned didn't look convinced. 'I think Sarah sees it different.'

'No, she doesn't. She's not interested in me.'

'She talks to you like she's real interested.'

'That's just Sarah being Sarah. The only reason I was accepted into her home was because *you* invited me. She told me.'

Ned scuffed a worn boot on the track ballast and looked down at the small crushed stones. 'What did Sarah say? You know, about me?'

'Well, she said …' Frank was searching for the right words.

'What?'

'Well …' The words still weren't coming.

Ned waited.

Frank gave up his quest. 'She said you were a fool. She said all men are fools when it comes to women.'

'So I'm a fool?' Ned was indignant.

'Yes, but you're her fool …' Frank screwed up his nose. 'That's not what I meant to say. I'm the idiot here, not you. Let me tell you straight. I am not making a play for Sarah.

I like her a lot, like if I had a smart big sister, but that's all.'

'She is smart, isn't she?'

Frank nodded.

'And she doesn't want you to take my place?'

'Definitely not. Just ask her.'

'I thought it was strange,' said Ned.

Frank's breathing had finally returned to normal and he relaxed. 'There you go, you knew.' Then Frank thought about what Ned had just said, and asked, 'Thought what was strange?'

'You and Sarah.'

'In what way?'

'You know.'

'No, not really.'

'You know, you and women.'

'What about me and women?'

'Well, you're not interested in women, are you?'

'What gives you that idea?'

'Well, you've never been with one.'

'Yes, I have.'

'I've never seen. When?'

'Well, a while ago now.'

'Before you went into prison?'

'Yes.' Frank's response was said with a tone of the obvious.

'So what did you do in prison?'

'I didn't do anything. Why, what did you think I did?'

'You hear stories.'

Frank pressed his lips together and shook his head. 'Well, they're not my stories.'

'It does happen, though, doesn't it? You know, between men? I mean, you hear stories.'

'Yeah, I've heard those stories. But I just stayed clear of

that sort of thing.'

'Did you hanker for it while you were in jail?'

Frank was getting really annoyed. 'For what exactly, Ned?'

'Being with a woman.'

Frank thought about it for a while and calmed down. 'No, not really. I had other things on my mind.'

'Like what?'

'Just trying to make it through each day and not think about how many more days I had in front of me.'

Ned's tone softened. 'Was it tough?'

'It was at first,' confessed Frank. 'I got a little angry. But what can you do? You just have to make a fist of it. That's life, isn't it?'

'Yeah, I guess,' said Ned, before adding, 'I don't think about it much, either.'

'Well, you don't have to, you have Sarah.'

'Yeah, but I think Sarah thinks about it a lot.'

'Really?' asked Frank with interest.

'I think so. Do you think I should think about it more?'

'Hell, Ned, I don't know, I'm no ladies' man.'

'Truth is, I need Sarah more than she needs me. I was in a bad way when you were put away. I thought it was my fault.'

'How so?' Frank was genuinely concerned.

'I should have given you an alibi.'

'How could you? They would have found it to be false. Besides, it wouldn't have made any difference. I was the one they wanted, and heaven and hell would not have made any difference.'

'Why?'

'Well, I always thought it was just payback for getting away with the first heist, but Sarah's got me thinking that there may be more to it.' Frank's shoulder's sagged. 'Ned, I didn't mean to come between you and Sarah. I guess I wasn't respecting you. Maybe I should move out.'

'Where to?'

'I don't know, but I just sort of arrived on your doorstep and Sarah let me in. I didn't even ask.'

'I asked for you, and she said yes. She expected it. We talked about you a lot. I told her everything, about our jobs, and Todd. She never passed a word on to anyone else. You can trust Sarah.'

'I know that.'

Ned reached out and touched Frank's arm. 'And I didn't mean to insult you.'

'Insult me?'

'You know, about not liking women.'

'That's OK,' said Frank.

'So, when were you last with a woman?' asked Ned with more than a touch of curiosity.

Frank was a bit sheepish. 'About a year before I went inside.'

'Where?'

'Here, Kanas City, down by the river, at night.'

'Did you do it?'

Frank was embarrassed. 'Yes, sort of, but I kept worrying I was going to get something.'

'Like what?'

'You know, a disease.'

'Why did you think that?'

'Well, I was paying for it. And you hear stories when you pay for it. You know, getting things from other men they have been with.'

Ned nodded. 'Did you?'

'Did I what?'

'Get a disease?'

'No, but I was sure I was going to.'

'Was she nice, though?'

Frank became business-like. 'Yes, she was nice.' Then he relaxed. 'She smelt nice. And she was nice to hold.'

'Do you think of her?'

'Every now and then, when I wonder what it would be like, you know, like you and Sarah.'

Ned reflected. 'It is good, and maybe I went a little crazy in the head thinking it had all gone.'

'Just a little crazy?' questioned Frank.

'Yeah, like you.'

'I'm not crazy.'

Ned's look was now questioning.

'Maybe once I was, but not any more, Ned. I've had the wind knocked out of me too many times to get crazy any more.'

'Well, maybe you need to get some of that wind back.'

'Why?'

'Because that's how you used to get things done.'

15

WITNESS

Confrontation in Missouri

When Frank and Ned returned to Stilwell, they had already discussed and made plans to go to Lee's Summit and find

Samuel Davidson. They even contemplated doing it while still at the junction as the settlement was only twenty-four miles out of Kansas City. It was on the Missouri Pacific line to St. Louis and would be a simple ride if they were to jump on an eastbound freight there and then. But Frank knew the importance of returning Ned to Sarah and fixing the misunderstanding first. Once reunited and with her blessing, they would go to Lee's Summit.

Later that evening, with visible relief to all, the subject changed from one of Ned's bruised feelings to future proceedings. Sarah was told of their plan to confront the mail van clerk who had falsely identified Frank as the perpetrator of the second heist.

Her immediate response was, 'I want to go, too.'

'No,' said Ned. 'It could be dangerous.'

Frank watched Sarah who was just about to protest when she looked at Ned and said softly, 'Very well, dear.'

Sarah's instant change of demeanour, however, was not totally convincing as Frank observed that her words and tone didn't match the look in her eyes. How smart, he thought. She has just read Ned like a book and made him feel like a king. How do women do that?

'But tell me,' said Sarah with a touch of firmness, 'what are you going to say to Samuel Davidson?'

'You mean with my loaded gun?' asked Frank.

'Yes,' said Sarah. 'If you have him looking down the barrel of a loaded gun, then he will be fearful and admit his guilt.'

'So you want that I should threaten him?' asked Frank

'If you want him to talk.'

'Where do you get such notions?' asked Ned.

'Sherlock Holmes,' replied Sarah.

'Who?'

'He's a detective.' Sarah went over to her knitting basket and pulled out a well-read copy of *Beeton's Christmas Annual* and held it up.

'A magazine detective?' came the surprised response from Frank.

'What, like Pinkerton?' questioned Ned.

Frank took the magazine from Sarah and began to flick through the pages and look at the illustrations. 'Does he carry a gun?'

'Yes, I think so.'

'With or without bullets?'

Sarah became annoyed. 'You are being churlish.'

'I'm being practical,' said Frank.

'Of course with bullets.' Sarah lifted her head to point a defiant nose in the air. 'They have the tenacity of bulldogs.'

'They?' said Frank and Ned together.

'Holmes and his companion, Dr Watson.'

Frank had to ask, 'He has his own doctor?'

'Watson is a long and cherished companion. Together they are Holmes and Watson.' Then Sarah added, 'Like Nester and Wilson.'

The comparison stopped both Frank and Ned in their tracks.

'The things you gals read,' said Frank.

'Yes, and maybe you should read them, too. Reading expands the mind.' Sarah snatched back the magazine.

'I'm sure we'll think of something to say, won't we, Ned?' said Frank in an effort to get the conversation back onto an even keel.

Ned quickly agreed. 'Yes, of course we will.'

Frank and Ned didn't get to Lee's Summit until the

following week. The necessity of chores around the property became the priority when some strong winds came through overnight and blew down a large old tulip tree that obstructed the track to and from the road.

The delay also caused the three of them to take the opportunity to discuss the best course of action. The chat had started over money. A little more than $100 now remained from what Sarah called the red barn money, and the prospect of getting any more by good or devious means was dim. Frank also had doubts if going after Sam Davidson still made any sense. What if he just repeated the same story he had told the court? Would threatening him really make a difference?

But Sarah was insistent. 'A lot of money has disappeared and someone knows where. Even if there is only some of it left, you should get your share for being jailed for twelve years.'

Ned said, 'Sounds fair.'

Sarah's response surprised Frank when she said, 'Fair has nothing to do with it. This is business.' She looked at Frank. 'You have been involved in their dirty, double deal and they need to pay you back for your services.'

Sarah had a way with words, which could have come from her detective magazine, but Frank had to admit that it seemed to make sense. 'But who are *they*?' he asked.

'That is why we have a list,' said Sarah, 'so we can find out, and Sam Davidson may well know. After all, he was a witness at your trial and swore under oath that it was you who committed the robbery. Therefore, was he mistaken or did he outright lie? Or was he threatened or was he paid from a robber's purse?'

Frank was feeling a little lost. 'And just what should I say when I find and confront Davidson?'

'You ask him to tell you everything about the events leading up to, during and after the robbery, and you do it in such a way as to make him feel obliged to tell you.'

'And that means threaten him?' said Ned, seeking confirmation.

Sarah nodded. 'You need to act like desperate men and put the very fear of the Lord into him.'

Frank was now starting to get a little worried. His previous thoughts on just how smart Sarah was when it came to the ways of the world seemed less so now that he knew they had come from an illustrated magazine. But he held his concerns at bay and said, 'OK, suppose he gives us names and places, then what?'

'You take note, come back here and tell me, and I will transcribe them. Then we will discuss them.'

Frank scratched his head. 'With respect, Sarah, this all sounds very clerical and I have trouble seeing where it will lead. Just say Davidson admits that he lied, then what?'

Sarah was getting a little frustrated, much like a schoolteacher with dim students. 'We already know that he lied, but we don't know why. And we don't know who got him to lie or if he was paid to lie. If we know who, then we get close to finding the money.'

Ned and Frank nodded in unison as they had to admit she had a point.

'Now, wash up for dinner. You both should have an early night. You leave for Lee's Summit before dawn.'

Lee's Summit had been built as a railroad settlement for watering the locomotives and maintaining the track. However, over time it had grown into a small commercial centre. It straddled the line with a main street either side but it was no metropolis. The plan for finding Davidson was to start at the station then move on out to the local businesses. Sarah suggested that they leave the saloon alone and ask at the general store or maybe the bakery, if the station agent didn't know. She also said as they departed, 'Be careful that you don't raise suspicions. You don't want him to run and hide.'

Frank and Ned jumped the early morning freight up to the junction. From there they purchased tickets to Lee's Summit. This was Sarah's idea as she said that they should arrive as paying passengers and present themselves as men of business. She even brushed their trousers and hung their coats overnight so that they would look presentable.

'And make sure you brush the seat of your pants when you get off at the junction and before you buy your rail tickets,' she instructed.

They both gave a *yes, ma'am* nod and guessed that such directions were common with English detectives.

They were at Lee's Summit by noon and it was Ned who approached a railway clerk standing at the end of the station and asked if he knew of a Mr Davidson who was believed to be a resident of the town.

The clerk seemed surprised and took a moment to gather his thoughts, saying that he was new in town himself and had not heard that name.

Ned repeated the name in full. 'Mr Samuel Davidson.' Then said, 'Maybe I could speak to the station agent?'

'He's busy, but I can speak to him for you if you would like to wait.'

Ned told him that was neighbourly and walked back to Frank who was at the other end of the station and told him what had transpired. They then sat down on one of the empty benches in the sun and waited.

After more than twenty minutes of enjoying the warmth, Ned said that he would go and find out what was the delay.

He returned to Frank in a rush. 'It was him. It was Davidson who I was talking to. I didn't recognize him.'

Frank had only seen the clerk from a distance. 'Are you sure? The man you were talking to was porky, real porky. Davidson wasn't that porky.'

'The station agent just told me that was him.'

Frank wasn't convinced. 'Where is he now?'

'Gone. The agent said he rushed off about half an hour ago.'

'He's done a runner?'

'Yeah.'

'Shit.' The profanity seemed to spit from between Frank's clenched teeth. 'It must have been him then.'

'Sorry, Frank, I should have recognized him from the trial ...'

Frank quickly tapped a hand against the side of Ned's shoulder to quieten him. 'No matter, he can't be too far away. Does the station agent know where he's gone?'

'No. But he saw him skedaddle without leaving a word.'

'We need to ask where he lives.'

'I did. He said on Douglas Street, two blocks over, near the general store. But he wanted to know why before he would tell me.'

'What did you say?'

'I said he owes us money.'

'What did the station agent say?'

'He just said, that figures.'

When Frank and Ned got to Douglas Street, they could see the sign for the general store but were confused as to where Davidson might have gone. Frank was about to ask in the store when he saw smoke coming from behind a small building just back from the street that looked a little like a shed for farm implements. They made their way around to the back of the store where an empty wagon was standing. Frank stood upon the wheel hub and looked over the next door fence and there was his man, the porky Samuel Davidson feverishly throwing papers into a small upright incinerator.

'It's him,' whispered Frank to Ned. 'Give me a leg up over the fence.'

On the count of three Frank went over the fence like a jack rabbit. Davidson looked up and let out a cry of anguish and threw a bundle of papers into the burner. Frank bolted for his man and caught him by the scruff of the neck.

'What are you up to, Davidson?' he shouted at the cringing figure.

Davidson seemed to lose all strength in his legs and buckled to a kneeling position.

'I knew you'd come one day. That you'd be out after twelve years and come looking for me.'

'And now I'm here so you better do some talking.' Frank was trying to remember what the questions were that Sarah said he should ask.

'I'll tell,' said the pleading Davidson. 'But you have to protect me. I need protection.'

'Why should I protect you, you lying rat?' Frank remembered that Sarah had called him a rat at one point.

'I didn't have a choice, I swear. It was more than my life if I didn't say that you robbed the train.'

'Then who was it that you saw in the mail van?'

'No one.'

Frank was ready to knuckle Davidson on the top of the head. 'What do you mean, "no one"? Someone robbed the train.'

'It wasn't like that at all. I just had to say it was you. The mail van wasn't robbed.'

Frank could feel his annoyance starting to rise. 'You're weasel wording me, Davidson.'

'No, I'm not. I can show you.'

'How?'

'Inside.'

'Where inside?'

'Where I sleep.'

Ned had scaled the fence at the corner post and dropped to the ground. 'You OK, Frank?'

'No, not until this weasel starts talking some sense, I'm not.' Frank pulled on Davidson's collar to lift him upright. 'Come on then, show me.'

When Davidson finally got to his feet, Ned noticed that their man had wet himself. 'Frank,' he said quietly and glanced to Davidson's crotch.

'What?' said Frank.

Ned glanced again and Frank finally looked down and saw. 'Go and clean yourself up, then we can talk. But don't you try and bolt out the front door. My gun is loaded.'

'I won't. I knew it would come to this and I'm ready.'

'Yeah, well, I'm ready, too, so don't take too long to put on a dry pair of trousers.'

When the three entered the hut it was dark and dank with a small room and a door to the front street.

'Ned, go and stand by the front door just in case.'

'I'm not leaving here,' said Davidson. 'And it is just one room. I will have no privacy when changing.'

'I'm not interested,' said Frank as Ned passed by towards the front door. 'I'm going to stand here.'

Samuel Davidson waddled across to the frame of a rusty metal cot in the corner of the room. Stacked alongside were two packing boxes with some books and a small oil lamp. Frank watched as Davidson leant against the makeshift shelving and with difficulty pulled off his boots, each falling to the floor with a clump. He then started to remove his trousers slowly to expose his large white flabby buttocks.

Frank looked over at Ned who shifted his weight from one foot to the other before they both turned their backs on the pathetic scene. But what was a small act of civility and privacy came at a terrible cost, for Frank and Ned had dropped their guard.

The shot from the pistol echoed like thunder in the small room. Frank instinctively gripped at his old cavalry holster and for a dreadful moment thought that Davidson had taken a shot at Ned. But as soon as he spun to turn and look, he realized immediately what had happened.

Davidson's body had collapsed to the floor with his trousers still around his knees and a bullet hole to his head where he had placed the barrel of a pistol directly above the bridge of his nose.

'Holy shit,' said Ned. 'He's shot himself.'

Frank leapt over to the body and dropped down on all fours and looked closely at Davidson's face in the poor light.

'Shit, shit, shit,' he said aloud. 'This is bad, Ned, real bad. We've got to get out of here, and we've got to do it quick. If we get caught here in Missouri we'll be charged with murder and never see Kansas again.'

16

LIKE BROTHER AND SISTER

Stilwell

Sarah woke from a light sleep when she heard Ned and Frank's footsteps upon the front porch. They were inside the house by the time she called out and joined them in the front room with a lit oil lamp. The golden glow that gently dispelled the dark did nothing to soften the concern on their faces.

'What is it?' she asked.

Ned looked at Frank, gesturing for him to tell her.

'Trouble,' is all he said.

Sarah put the lamp down on the table and pulled her shawl tight around her shoulders. 'Bad trouble?' she asked.

'Davidson is dead.'

'Oh my god, you shot him?'

'No,' said Frank, 'he shot himself, but we were there when he did it, so we're mixed up in it, like it or not.'

Sarah's face showed her shock. 'Why would he do such a thing?'

'We can't makes sense of it,' said Ned. 'We talked about it over and over on the ride back, but we can't figure.'

'And you think you could be blamed?'

Frank nodded with glum resignation. 'We arrived at the station, asked where he lived, he took off, and we followed after him. The next minute he is dead. I could see a sheriff adding this one up in a second.'

'But were you recognized?'

'The station agent saw our faces and he could identify us in a court. And Ned told him we were after Davidson for money owing.'

'I see,' said Sarah, uneasily to herself. 'Time, place and motivation.'

'Me and Ned may need to go and hide for a while. Maybe down south.'

'Then what?' The look on Sarah's face and the tone of her voice showed that she thought hiding didn't make sense.

Frank rubbed his chin. 'Till this blows over.'

Sarah shook her head. 'That's no plan. It's just running away and hoping.'

'We can talk about it in the morning,' said Frank.

'No,' said Sarah firmly. 'We need to talk about it now, while it is fresh in your minds and make a decision, a plan, one that can be acted on at first light. I need my book and pencil.'

'Not now,' said Ned.

But Sarah was insistent. 'Yes, now. We may have little time to act before the authorities come looking for you both.'

Frank conceded. 'Sarah is right, Ned. The only thing we have on our side at the moment is time and that is ticking away by the minute. And there has to be something we can do. It's just that I don't know what.'

Sarah returned from the kitchen with her recipe book and opened it to a fresh clean page. 'Tell me all of the events in order and slowly while I make notes.' She looked up. 'Well, sit down, we have work to do.'

Ned began from the time they had left that morning and journeyed to Kansas City and on to Lee's Summit. She quizzed each of them on every small detail and it surprised

Frank as to how much he had not considered. In the commotion of their escape, his mind had erratically jumped between what had happened in Davidson's hut and what they needed to do to safely get away.

Sarah thought that the burning of papers in the incinerator was most significant, but Frank and Ned had no inkling as to their importance. She also dwelled on Davidson's call for protection, along with questions on his dress, demeanour, conversation and subterfuge that allowed him to get to his gun. And by the time they had finally answered each and every question, the first glimmer of light was making its way into the room.

Sarah tucked the pencil behind her ear and examined her notes, before announcing, 'You had no choice but to confront and surprise Davidson. He knew you were innocent, Frank.'

'He was certainly surprised when he saw Frank, he was frightened half to death,' said Ned, before he realized what he had just said. 'Well, frightened a lot, wetting himself and all.'

'Did he do that?' asked Sarah.

Ned nodded.

Sarah removed her pencil from its perch and made a note. 'But exactly why was he so frightened that he would kill himself? If he thought you were going to kill him, why not fire his gun at both of you?'

Frank pondered Sarah's question before saying, 'He has carried those reasons to his grave.'

Sarah chewed on the end of her pencil in deep thought. 'Why would a man be so scared that he would rather take his life than live and face that fear?'

The room was silent as Sarah put the pencil down into

the fold of the book and closed it. She was starting to stand when Frank said, 'I know.'

Sarah sat back down, 'You do?'

'Yes,' said Frank as he stared at the morning light peeking through the kitchen window. 'I never got to see a sunrise for twelve years. My cell was on the west side. I have always loved dawn's first gleaming from the time I was a kid. My mother did, too. I would try and get up before her and stoke the stove so it was warm for her when she got up. She once said that my help on a cold winter's morning was better than any gift I could give her.'

Ned and Sarah sat silently observing Frank as the light glowed upon the features of his face.

'If I had to go back to that cell on the west side of Lansing, I'd shoot myself in an instant, just like Davidson.'

Sarah held her breath before she asked, 'But what was it for Davidson? He'd never been to prison.'

'Something similar, but I don't know what,' said Frank.

'Or was it someone?' said Sarah. 'Was he in fear of someone? Was he seeking protection from someone, not something?'

'Whatever it was,' said Frank, 'he knew that I couldn't shield him.'

'But to do what he did, and so quickly, without hesitation, he must have been living in constant fear.' Sarah drew in a long nervous breath. 'I should have left all of this well alone, shouldn't I?'

Frank half grinned but did not take his eyes from the morning light as it glowed stronger through the window. 'I should have led a better life. I should have made my mother proud. I was a first class idiot. But what's done is done, and if there is only one thing that I know for sure, it's that I'm not going back inside. Not for no one. No time.'

'What do we do now?' asked Ned.

Sarah gathered her composure and looked down at her recipe book and calmed herself by reading out her notes. 'Davidson was adamant that the mail van wasn't robbed. He said that he was going to show you something to prove it, but all he had to do was just tell you. He wanted time to get to his gun. This was a decision that he had considered in advance.'

Frank and Ned listened.

'Is it possible?' said Sarah as she made a quick, pencilled notation. 'Just as Davidson said, that the van wasn't robbed? What if the money wasn't taken off the train at Spring Hill, but that it travelled on up to Kansas City in the mail van with Davidson?'

Frank looked over at Sarah, who was doing that familiar tapping thing of the pencil against her cheek again, and said, 'What would your magazine detective say to that?'

Sarah looked up, embarrassed. 'Oh, that's just magazine poppycock.'

Frank half smiled. 'But would your detective be brave enough to pursue the very idea that someone inside the Missouri Pacific Railroad took the money from the safe when the train arrived in Kansas City?'

'Well,' said Sarah gingerly, 'he would determine who had access to the van on arrival.'

'But would Davidson still be on board?' asked Ned.

'Why not?' said Frank. 'Davidson was their man escorting the money.'

'Who would normally receive the money once it got to Kansas City?' asked Sarah. 'The bank?'

Frank nodded. 'The money was from the McAlester Cattle Yards, so I expect the bank would collect it on arrival.'

'But they are going to be told that the money has been stolen,' said Sarah. 'So there is nothing there for them to collect.'

'True,' said Frank.

'So the police would be called,' said Sarah.

'Of course,' said Frank. 'The police.'

'Have the police taken the money, then?' asked Ned.

'Yes, no, not the police from Kansas City, but the railroad police.' Frank had a look of enlightenment upon his face. 'They would do their own investigation and then report the robbery to the Kansas City Police. And that investigation would be the job of Rodney D. Dodd, Special Agent of the Missouri Pacific Railroad Police Department.'

Sarah was getting excited. 'And it was Dodd who then arrested you, saying the crime was exactly like the previous heist two years before.' She was now frantically flicking the pages in her book. 'We need to find Dodd, but we don't know where he is. Only that someone down at the station said they thought he was still working for the railroad up in Kansas City.'

'Or do we wait? Maybe Dodd is going to come looking for me,' said Frank.

'Why?' asked Ned.

'For the murder of Samuel Davidson. Then he'd really have me at the end of rope.'

'But why would you want to kill Davidson?' asked Sarah.

'Revenge, and there was a time when I thought about it, I can tell you.'

'So do we wait?' asked Ned.

'No,' said Frank. 'I'm not going to be trapped this time. Sarah is right. I need to find Dodd first, before he finds me. A warrant for my arrest will take me back to Missouri to face a murder trial.'

Sarah shifted in her chair and pulled her wrap around her shoulders against the morning chill. 'Frank, that's too dangerous for you and Ned to go looking for Dodd.'

'I'll go on my own.'

Sarah straightened her back. 'No, you can't. You will have no one to assist you. Ned can stay here. I'll go with you.'

'Why you?' asked Frank, 'but not Ned?'

'If Dodd and the authorities are looking, they won't be searching for a man and a woman together. And if I enquire about the whereabouts of Mr Dodd, then it may not raise suspicion.' Sarah turned to Ned. 'However, I will only go with your permission, Edward.'

'Edward,' mumbled Ned to himself. He hadn't been called Edward since his christening. However, he instantly warmed to the formality of the title and looked over at Sarah, and slowly nodded his head. 'You could go as family, like brother and sister.'

Sarah nodded back in agreement, while Frank watched on and pressed a finger to his lips, as if to stop even one word from passing.

17

LOOKING FOR DODD

Kansas City

Sarah was giving a dismissive tut-tut quietly as she read the *Kansas City Journal*.

Frank glanced over at the page.

'Two dollars for ladies shoes,' she said in an annoyed tone. 'Tell me, who can afford that? Look there.' Her head turned as she pointed her nose to the other page. 'You can buy a rocking chair from Buchanan's for $1.58. I see far better value in a chair than shoes.'

Frank wasn't sure if this was a conversation or a sermon. 'Unless you have bare feet,' he ventured.

An older woman in the facing seat leant forward towards Sarah, glanced at Frank, and in sympathy said, 'That's exactly what my husband would say.'

Frank was about to correct the woman in regard to their pretend relationship as siblings, when Sarah said, 'Yes, I know. Husbands are all the same when it comes to the business of home and garden.'

The new acquaintance nodded in agreement while Frank accepted that he had not been invited into this discussion. Maybe it was best to remain mute. He looked across at the young boy sitting next to the woman. He was cradling the left side of his face in his palm.

'Tooth?' asked Frank.

The boy nodded.

'My grandson,' said the woman. 'I'm taking him to the dentist in Topeka. A wonderful man. Did his father's teeth when he was just a boy. Cost us a fortune, but worth every penny. Good teeth are important.'

Frank and the boy looked at each other in sober silence while gently swaying to the rhythm of the carriage and listening to the clack of the wheels on the steel rails. They were fellow travellers in the care of women.

Sarah turned the page. Frank glanced over and watched her head lean in to examine the print closely. It was too early to report the death of Samuel Davidson, but sure enough, it would be in the journal before week's end. Frank looked to see what had now taken Sarah's interest and saw that she was reading an advertisement for pianos. It said: *New designs for the new centenary. 1900 pianos at the lowest prices. We have upright pianos at $150. F. G. Smith Western Warerooms on Walnut.* Sarah was so engrossed that she made a sudden little jolt when the whistle blew and the train began to slow.

'Right on time,' said the woman opposite as she opened the clasp on a small gold pocket watch.

'You have your own timepiece?' asked Sarah with interest.

'I do. It was an anniversary present from my husband. He's in banking.'

'May I see?'

The woman handed it over with a smile and Sarah took it carefully. 'Beautiful,' she said as her gloved hand brushed a finger across the embossed case.

When the woman and her grandson had alighted and Sarah and Frank were walking down the platform, Frank felt a tug on his sleeve.

'Did you see the shine of the gold on that timepiece? And taking children to a dentist in Topeka. How do people afford such wealthy pursuits?'

'Didn't you hear? Her husband was in banking.'

'There is another world out there, isn't there? But just how do you think they get to belong to it? Is it just hard work? I've worked hard all my life, and look at us, you, me and Ned. We're like church mice.'

'Maybe you've got to be born into it, or maybe it's luck,' said Frank.

'Isn't luck the same as opportunity?' said Sarah.

'I guess we all hope it is,' said Frank. 'But where do

people like us find opportunity?'

'Well, if I ever got the opportunity to be rich, I would take it with both hands and never let go,' said Sarah, turning her hands palm up as she spoke and splaying the fingers, only to quickly close them again on noticing a small hole in the well-worn glove at the tip of her right middle finger.

When they got to the Union Depot gate, the station was busy with the noise and bustle of passengers arriving and departing, and that was how Frank wanted it to be so that they could hide in the crowd. Maybe not as brother and sister as originally intended, but now as man and wife.

The Kansas City office of the Missouri Pacific Railroad was a little further down on Union Avenue, so said the ticket collector. The sign on the entrance said *Enquiries This Way* and looked official rather than welcoming. Frank opened the door for Sarah, then stepped back to wait outside as they had arranged.

When she returned, it was with the news that no one had heard of an employee named Dodd, but that they should try further down at the door marked *Vacancies* as it was there that they held the list of names for all current employees.

'If Dodd was still working for the Missouri Pacific, they would know,' said Sarah.

The last thing Frank desired was a surprised confrontation with Dodd. He just wanted to know his whereabouts, then select a time and place of his own choosing. However, he was now somewhat confident that the chance of coming face to face was unlikely, so he told Sarah that he would make the enquiry.

The junior clerk behind the desk thrust a job application under Frank's nose before he had even opened his mouth. He waved it away and asked if he could check the employee roll. The clerk advised that he would have to see his superior and because today was the first Tuesday of the month, he would be in Topeka and not back till Thursday.

It was on walking back down the panelled corridor that Frank glanced up and saw the polished honour boards. It listed the names of those who had provided distinguished service. He paused mid-step, turned and looked again as he scanned the names, and there, three quarters down the list was the name Dodd. He stepped back to read it in full. It said, *Rodney D. Dodd 1866–1888*, and it was as if Frank was actually in the presence of the railway detective once again, just as a voice behind him said, 'Impressive bit of wood that. Varnished oak with gold leaf lettering.'

Frank had to regain his composure before he turned to see an old man clutching a broom. 'Nice,' he said to the janitor. 'I guess you get to keep it polished up.'

'Once a month. Doesn't need much. No oil, just a cap of wax, no more, and a good cloth.'

'Yes, a good cloth,' repeated Frank in small talk as he turned to leave, when the thought crossed his mind. 'Did you know any these men?'

'Sure, I goes back a way.'

'As far as '88?'

'And some.'

'Dodd? That name rings a bell, but I can't recall why. Did you know him?'

'I knowed of him, but no, I didn't know him. Detective Dodd made a name for himself when he solved the Spring Hill heists. Big news back then. Did it single-handed.'

'But he's no longer with the railway, is that right?'

'Left to work in Topeka in '88.'

'Still there?' asked Frank.

'Guess.'

Frank tried not to rush the slow conversation should his questions sound anything but casual 'With another railway?'

'No, he was a Missouri Pacific man through and through. No other railroad for him.'

Frank now tried to slow his mind down so that he didn't jump to conclusions. He could hear his head saying, what would Sarah's detective say? So he took in a measured breath. 'So why did he give up working for the Missouri Pacific, then?'

'Got a job working with the government. That's why he went to Topeka.'

Frank nodded his head wisely. 'Doing what?'

'Government work.'

Frank nodded wisely again as he said, 'Government work, right. Must have been a smart man, being able to do railroad work and government work.'

'Missouri Pacific got lots of smart men,' said the janitor.

Frank could think of nothing to say so he just continued nodding his head.

'Just like Senator Richard Jenkins. Got his name on a notice board, too.'

Frank nearly choked when he heard the name Jenkins. 'Senator Jenkins,' he sputtered. 'You should show me.'

He was taken back up the corridor and there on another polished board was the name Richard Jenkins 1870–1888. 'They both left in 1888,' observed Frank.

'Yep.'

'Coincidence, I guess,' said Frank.

'Nope.'

'Why is that?'

The janitor kept looking up at the name. 'Well, them

being together and all, it was more predictable than coincidence.'

'Predictable? Why predictable more than coincidence?' asked Frank.

'The stories.'

'What stories?'

'Well, I don't like telling stories 'bout names in such fine lettering. Gold leaf and all.'

'No, of course,' said Frank. 'Being gold leaf.'

'Expensive gold leaf.'

Frank nodded in agreement.

'But words have been said.'

Frank had no idea what the janitor was talking about, so he just said, 'Yes, they certainly have.'

The janitor looked at Frank. 'So you've heard them, too?'

Frank just kept looking up at the gold leaf name of Jenkins. 'I've heard some,' he said.

'All that smoke, bound to be some fire.'

'Well, that's usually my experience,' said Frank.

'Mine, too. So them going together, up to Topeka, to work together, well, it was just predictable, wasn't it?'

Frank had to almost bite his tongue to stop from saying aloud, 'They are working together? They went to Topeka to work together?'

When he saw Sarah back out on the street near a fruit stall, it was with an apple in her hand. 'You want a bite?' she asked.

Frank's words tumbled out at such speed that she had to ask him to repeat them. He did. 'Did you see when the next train leaves for Topeka?'

'No, why?' Sarah had taken a bite and had to ask why with her mouth full, while holding a hand to her lips.

'Dodd is in Topeka?'

She swallowed quickly. 'You have an address?'

'No.'

'How are we going to find him?'

'By finding Senator Jenkins.'

'He is with Senator Jenkins?'

'Seems so.'

'Doing what?'

'I'm not sure, but it all seems to involve some sort of smoke and fire.'

'Smoke?' questioned Sarah. 'What sort of smoke?'

'I have no idea,' said Frank, 'but whatever it is, it has got people talking about them being together since '88.'

'Since 88?' said Sarah.

'Yes,' said Frank. 'Something about being predictable more than coincidence.'

'Oh, that,' said Sarah knowingly.

'What?'

'You know.'

'No, I don't know,' said Frank. 'I haven't the foggiest.'

'You know. A man's impropriety with another man.'

Frank's brow furrowed. 'What sort of impropriety?'

Sarah took another small bite of her apple, then looked down the street as she spoke. 'You know, men, going together in private with each other, sort of impropriety.'

'Oh,' said Frank, nodding his head and feeling a little embarrassed. 'That sort of impropriety.'

Sarah looked around again to make sure that no one was in earshot and lowered her voice. 'So what did you hear, exactly?'

'Well, I saw their names on a wallboard and they both left in '88 together, and Dodd now works for the Senator.'

'Well, that is most interesting,' said Sarah.

'Well, yes, it is,' said Frank. Then he thought about it and he wasn't sure exactly why it was most interesting. He went to ask Sarah for clarification, but stopped short and asked instead, 'Will I need my gun?'

Sarah had finished her apple and was examining the core. 'I wouldn't think so but best to keep it handy, just in case.'

18

DEMOCRACY

Topeka

Topeka was unfamiliar to Frank and Sarah, but the Kansas State Capitol building dominated the skyline and not only gave them direction from afar, but contributed to a feeling of the prominence and importance of government.

'Should we even be here?' Sarah asked Frank.

He wasn't sure what she actually meant. 'If you are asking me where all this is leading to, I have no idea. If you are saying should we be here trying to find the truth, then why shouldn't we? We are Kansas citizens going to see a Kansas senator. And isn't this where democracy sits?'

'What has democracy got to do with the likes of us?' said Sarah. 'I don't get to vote. Do you, Frank?'

'Not after doing jail time.'

'I don't know if I even understand democracy.'

'You understand liberty and truth better than anyone I

know,' said Frank.

'But do we get that from democracy?'

'Supposed to.'

Sarah thought about it for a second or two. 'Where did you learn that from?'

'My mother.'

Sarah was silent for a moment or two before asking, 'You miss her?'

'I try not to, but she keeps coming back in dreams lately,' said Frank without any sense of awkwardness.

Sarah felt a little embarrassed for having asked such a personal question and patted Frank's arm gently as they looked up at the dome of the Capitol.

'Do we just go inside and ask for Senator Jenkins?'

'Guess so,' said Frank.

'What do we say if we are asked why?'

Frank shrugged. 'That we would like to discuss some e-lec-tor-rial business.'

'What sort of e-lec-tor-rial business?'

'Geez, I don't know, Sarah. Just some business, then.'

'Better leave this to me, Frank,' said Sarah as she began to walk to the entrance.

Frank followed a pace or two behind up the wide stone steps, but Sarah was getting away from him. She seemed to have a purpose in every stride.

At the top, in between the towering columns, Sarah engaged a gentleman as he was leaving and about to descend the steps. Frank couldn't hear what was being said, but the accosted man pointed inside. Sarah took off again at a brisk pace in the direction given.

When Frank did catch up, Sarah was at a large desk and asking politely for the whereabouts of Senator Jenkins.

The clerk looked concerned. 'Did you have an appointment?'

'No,' said Sarah.

The clerk now looked a little relieved. 'Have you come far?'

'Stilwell.'

'I wish you'd come earlier,' he said.

'Why earlier? What's wrong with now? Are you going to tell me that the Senator is too busy to see me?'

'No, madam. The representatives look forward to meeting with all citizens. It is just that Senator Jenkins took leave to travel at short notice.'

'Oh,' said Sarah, as if the wind had been taken from her sails. 'So he's not here in Topeka?'

'No,' said the clerk. 'Not even in Kansas.'

Frank caught the clerk's eye. 'Where exactly did the Senator go?'

'Missouri, I believe. But I have no exact address.'

Frank could guess where, but he wanted to make sure.

'Did he go alone?'

'No, sir. He is travelling with his assistant.'

Frank smiled. 'And that would be Mr Dodd, I expect.'

Sarah quickly glanced at Frank then back at the clerk.

'Yes, sir, that's right. The Senator's senior assistant is Mr Dodd.'

'And Mr Dodd always travels with the Senator on business?'

'He does, sir.'

'Thank you,' said Frank as he extended his hand to the clerk.

'Who will I say has called when the Senator returns?' asked the clerk as he shook Frank's hand.

Frank held the clerk's grip. 'Tell him Frank Nester called. He will remember me.'

'Can I have your address in Stilwell so he may write?'

'No need.'

'Any message?'

Frank nearly said no, but he paused just long enough to consider. 'Yes, tell him that I'll be catching up with him and his senior assistant in the near future.' Frank released his grip on the clerk's hand and smiled.

When they walked away Sarah asked with concern, 'Why did you say that?'

'They have heard about Davidson and gone to Lee's Summit,' replied Frank.

'I gathered that, but why say that you were going to catch up with them in the near future?'

Frank was now at the top of the steps and he stopped to look down Ninth Street and Kansas Avenue.

'Grand, isn't it?' he said.

'Frank? Answer me,' she said with annoyance.

'They will be coming after me, but I want them to know that I'm coming after them. There's no going back now. This is heading for a showdown.'

'If it is a showdown, then they will win.'

'This is a most impressive view,' said Frank with a smile.

Sarah was now starting to get angry. 'Stop fussing about the view, Frank. We can't win a showdown.'

'I don't expect to, but if I go down, I will take them with me.'

'And how do you expect to do that?' asked Sarah.

Frank turned his head and looked at Sarah. 'With a loaded gun.'

The realization of what Frank was saying stunned her.

'That's suicide, Frank.'

'No,' he said. 'It is what it is. No more, no less. You fight with what you've got in the best way you've got.' Frank glanced over his shoulder at the State Capitol building. 'They have this, but I have a gun and that makes me equal, and democracy is about being equal. You know, not giving you the vote and taking it away from me in prison isn't about democracy, but keeping the likes of you and me in our place. Keeping us as little people.'

Sarah felt her blood run cold. 'Little, yes, but we are not outlaws, are we, Frank?'

'When you can't get justice, you may as well be. Because all the laws passed in this place are worth nothing without justice.'

A breath of wind passed across Sarah's face and she felt it on her dry lips. 'Hold my hand, Frank.'

Frank lifted his hand from his side and felt the cold of her ungloved fingers entwine and grip his.

'I'm frightened,' she said. 'Are you?'

'No, not any more.'

The way he said it reassured her.

'I refuse to go to my grave a timid man,' said Frank.

'I wish I had your strength.' Sarah seemed to shake as if a chill had passed down the length of her body.

'But you do,' said Frank without taking his eyes from the horizon. 'That's why men like me and Ned are drawn to women like you, Sarah.'

Sarah squeezed Frank's hand. 'Is it wrong if I want two men at once?'

Frank smiled as he looked straight ahead. 'Not if one of them is me.'

19

AN UNHOLY ALLIANCE

Topeka

The warmth of Frank's hand contrasted with the cold stark reality of the situation and left Sarah with a feeling of doom that churned deep in the pit of her stomach. As they walked side by side in silence back towards the station, she found her imagination whirling out of control. She could envisage Senator Jenkins parading into Stilwell ahead of Dodd and a gang of masked vigilantes hell bent on hanging Frank and burning her home to the ground.

By the time they arrived back at the Union Depot, she was emotionally exhausted and excused herself to the ladies' restroom to regain composure. But alone in the cubicle only made matters worse and she burst into tears. A knock from the adjoining stall was followed by a call to see if she was all right. Quickly, Sarah dried her eyes with the palms of her hands and wiped her nose on her sleeve.

'Fine, thank you,' she answered. But she wasn't and as she got up to leave, her beaded handbag caught on the small brass doorhandle and jerked from her grip. It hit the floor with a clump to spray small black embroidered beads upon the tiled floor. Desperately she tried to collect them in the palm of her hand, but grasping the runaway decorations from their hiding places was a futile affair. She snatched up her bag in defeat, saying 'Damn' just as the contents fell out of the upturned reticule. It was enough to cause the tears to flow again, along with more unladylike expletives as she tried to shovel the displaced items back where they belonged. The largest article in her bag was her recipe book, and when she went to pick it up, it fell again from her hand and landed, page open, to where she had pencilled in her list. There was the name of Fletcher Prowse looking up at her.

'Fletcher,' she said with muffled scorn. 'Such a silly name for a man, or for anyone for that matter. And where are you when needed, Fletcher? Dead, that's where you are. Frank is about to be killed, my house burnt down, and where are you? Dead.'

Some gentle taps knocked against the cubicle wall. 'Dear, are you sure you are all right?'

Damn fine and dandy, thought Sarah, but she said instead, 'Yes, thank you. Just dropped my bag.'

'You sound upset.'

Of course I'm upset, she thought. You would be too if the men in your life and your home were all going to be taken away.

'No, really, I'm fine,' she tried to respond with as much levity as she could muster while snatching up the book and looking at what she had written upon the page. *Daughter, Quincy Street, Topeka – compiling a book on her father's life and times. High priority.*

'Are you sure?'

'Really, I'm fine now.' said Sarah softly as she read the words again. 'Quincy Street.'

'What was that?'

'I said, Quincy Street. Do you know where Quincy Street is?'

'It's just behind Kansas Avenue, down from the Capitol.'

When Sarah returned to Frank, she was in a minor

fluster while he was a picture of cool composure as he leant up against the end of the station bench seat.

'I have our tickets,' he said. 'But the train doesn't leave for another two and a half hours.'

'It doesn't matter when it leaves,' said Sarah. 'We have to go back.'

'Back where?'

'Near the Capitol to Quincy Street.'

'Why?'

'To talk to the daughter of Fletcher Prowse.'

Frank sat down on the bench next to Sarah. 'What purpose would that do?'

'She is compiling a book, look.' Sarah dug into her frayed bag to drag out the recipe book. 'See, I wrote it down. Remember?'

Frank couldn't remember. 'When?'

'After I spoke to the clerk of the court in Stilwell. You remember, don't you?'

'Vaguely. Show me.' When Frank read what Sarah had written it did jog his memory a little, but he still failed to see the significance. 'So?'

'We need to know if she has discovered anything.'

'Like what?'

'Like...' Sarah seemed to do a little sitting jig and for a moment Frank wondered if she was going to stamp her feet. 'I don't know, but something. Something that might tell us that Jenkins and Dodd were involved in the robbery.'

'I have already deduced that,' said Frank.

'But you can't prove it. And in the story in *Beeton's Christmas Album*, proof is the necessary ingredient in the successful indictment of all crime.'

'Sarah, that's just a detective magazine.'

'It may be just a magazine, but what else do we have, and what are you going to do? Sit here like a stuffed turkey for two hours or more?'

Frank averted his eyes from Sarah's fierce gaze to see, with surprise, that the woman and the boy who had travelled up with them on the train were now sitting and watching from the opposite bench. The side of her grandson's face was puffy while her face looked hard and sour. She's just paid the dentist's bill, he thought. She was looking directly at Frank and examining him as if he was indeed a stuffed turkey. Frank immediately knew that anything would have to be better than sitting here right at this moment, let alone for the next couple of hours.

'Let's go,' he said and pushed himself up from the bench and began to walk to the exit.

Sarah glanced across and recognized the woman and boy, and gave a nod.

'Yes, dear,' she said and followed.

Had it not been for the old shingle that still hung from the front porch with the faded name proclaiming *F. Prowse, Attorney at Law*, then they might not have found his house.

Sarah knocked on the door while Frank waited at the front gate. When the door finally opened, it was by a straight-backed woman with her hair tied in a tight bun. Her greeting of, 'Yes?' was as forthright as her appearance.

'Are you Attorney Prowse's daughter?' asked Sarah.

The woman's head tilted back a little. 'I am.'

'I'm Sarah Lennon and—' But she was cut short.

'I'm not buying.'

'And I'm not selling,' responded Sarah abruptly.

'Then good day,' came the declaration as the door started to close.

'Hear her out,' called Frank with authority.

The woman reopened the door and took a step forward to look at Frank. 'Why?'

'We have come for your help,' he said.

'And who are you?' said the woman.

'I knew your father. He defended me in Stilwell in '87. He saved me from the rope.' Frank paused before he added, 'but at a price.'

The woman's stance changed immediately. Her shoulders dropped forward a little and the tone of her voice changed. 'Are you Frank Nester?'

'Yes, that's right.'

She drew in a quick breath and raised a hand to her neck. 'Frank Nester, how can it be?'

'Why can't it be?' asked Frank.

'You better come in, because you're supposed to be dead.'

When Sarah shuffled into the parlour of the house that Fletcher Prowse had built for his wife Rose, she saw a photograph of the young attorney with his wife and baby daughter Catherine wrapped in a white shawl.

'She died when I was eight,' said Catherine Prowse. 'I was their only child.'

'A handsome family,' said Sarah with keen curiosity as she perched herself on the edge of the parlour chair.

'It is my only memento of the three of us,' was the reply.

When Frank bent forward to see the picture it was not of the man he had known. This one was younger, keener, and prouder, but he could still see the resemblance and it brought back the memories. He looked up at the daughter. 'You thought I was dead?'

'I presumed.'

'What, that I had died in prison?'

'No, well, maybe. I don't know. My father said that they wanted you dead.'

'They?' asked Frank.

Sarah sat forward a little and asked, 'Who are they? The ones who put Frank in jail?'

'It was my father who put Mr Nester in jail. It was the only way he knew how to stop him from being hanged. But he said they would eventually get him if they were to keep their secret undisclosed.'

Sarah leant further forward and looked as if she was about to fall off. 'Who? What secret?'

'My father drew the conclusion that only those with privileged knowledge from within the Missouri Pacific could have planned and carried out such a large robbery. Especially, if they wanted it to look like a replica of Frank's earlier heist. And as each year passed his conviction firmed. He said the only mistake in the implementation of their plan was Frank going to jail and not the gallows.' Catherine fixed her eyes on Frank. 'My father always believed that assassins would kill you eventually. Either in jail or once released.'

'But who exactly?' asked Sarah. 'Did he give you any names?'

'He reasoned that every Missouri Pacific employee who had a direct involvement in the trial was under suspicion, until cleared.'

'Why the trial in particular?' asked Sarah.

'Because my father came to the conclusion that the trial was part of the robbery.'

Frank went to speak but on seeing Sarah on the edge of her seat, decided to leave the questions to her.

'He believed that it was an essential part of the robbery to put the blame on Frank as that would then ensure that the case was closed and leave those who perpetrated the deed in the clear.'

'That would have included Jenkins and Dodd,' said Sarah quietly.

Catherine nodded her agreement. 'However, my father was quick to point out that they should remain innocent until proven guilty. Well, at least he said that up until a year before his death. By then he wasn't too sure if they should be given the benefit of the doubt, especially when he'd had a drink or two. However, he was careful not to include their names in his notes. He worried that it would place both me and him at great risk.'

'Notes, what notes?' asked Sarah.

'My father was writing a book on all of his cases. There were many, but Frank's was of particular interest and importance to him.'

'How exactly?' questioned Sarah.

'Well, without putting too fine a point on it, he believed that the seeds of the second heist all came from the success of the first. Frank had not only stolen from the Missouri Pacific, but he had shown up certain individuals as being less than competent. This resulted in bad blood of which Frank was totally unaware. However, what may have been an idle idea to recover lost revenue and restore reputations through the staging of a replica heist, somehow turned into a major act of larceny for personal gain.'

Frank couldn't help but feel a little bewildered.

Sarah was nodding her head in agreement as she listened, while he dared not open his mouth in case he might embarrass himself.

'So your father believed that a plan was hatched to repeat the same heist.'

'Not precisely. Just to make it *appear* to be an exact imitation of the first heist.'

Sarah's brow creased. 'Make it appear?'

'Yes, my father was of the opinion that there was no second heist by bandits boarding the train. It was just a pretence, a charade, a farce. My father referred to it as theatrics.'

Frank drew in a long breath then expelled slowly. The two women looked at him. 'Samuel Davidson, the mail van clerk, told me as much himself before he died.'

The attorney's daughter was a little surprised. 'When did he die?'

'Yesterday.'

Her eyes widened. 'Did you kill him?'

'No. He committed suicide but I was there.'

'Oh dear, oh dear. My father always said that this was a most dangerous affair for all concerned. Does Jenkins and Dodd know of this?' she asked.

'We believe so,' said Sarah.

'But they don't know the circumstances or what he said to me,' said Frank. 'But they will think I did it.'

'My father always said that you would eventually figure this all out by yourself.'

Frank shook his head. 'Your father gives me more credence than I deserve. I've had to be led by the hand in getting this far.'

'But my father also felt that you would be no match against the likes of Dodd and Jenkins or anyone that was an accomplice. He said that they would bury you in an unmarked grave.'

In Frank's heart of hearts he knew she was probably right. It was just a matter of time. The only reason it hadn't happened before now was most likely because he'd been behind a prison wall.

The look on Sarah's face was intense. 'What evidence did your father have that linked Jenkins and Dodd to the train robbery?'

'Unfortunately, very little and he knew it. He wrote that it was suspicion based on events and timings, but disturbing suspicion none the less. His starting point was Dodd's grievance with Frank for making him look foolish.'

'And Jenkins?' asked Sarah. 'He was a man of the law.'

'A very ambitious man of the law who wanted to be a politician.'

'Which he achieved,' said Sarah.

'Yes, but only after he had received a large undisclosed contribution to his campaign fund. He practically bought his way into the office.'

Sarah's eyes widened in disbelief.

'My father said that he could feel injustice in his bones and that Frank was the innocent party.' Before adding, 'At least on this occasion.'

'Can we see what your father wrote?' asked Sarah.

'I'll show you. All my father's papers are in his study.'

The room was crowded with books and reams of paper piled high upon a small desk and on the floor. But there was a sense of order. The daughter pointed towards the tallest stack in the corner of the room next to the bookshelves. 'This is the one related to Frank's case.'

'Where should I start?' asked Sarah.

Catherine commenced to lift individual bundles of papers tied by coloured ribbon. 'On the top of the pile are the legal arguments. Below that are the facts of law, and finally the findings. But what you need to read is this.' She held up a leather bound notebook. 'My father wrote a mono-logue, which he titled *An Unholy Alliance*.'

Sarah was handed the notebook and she began to read, but stopped abruptly. 'No, this must be the wrong case. It is about a man called Dorrit.'

'Frank's name is not mentioned,' said the daughter. 'He was fearful that it would put him at risk—'

'Little Dorrit,' interrupted Frank. 'That's what he once called me.'

'Why?' asked Sarah.

Frank shrugged. 'I have no idea, other than telling me that the law is an idiot.'

'Little Dorrit is a character from the writer Charles Dickens. My father loved Dickens. I'm named after his wife, Catherine.'

Sarah returned to her reading in silence while Frank watched her examine each page with a serious expression before turning it slowly. She didn't speak for the best part of half an hour before saying, 'The handwriting has changed, here, is it yours?'

Catherine confirmed that it was.

'Who is Rupert?'

'It is the name of the newspaper man who covered Frank's trial. He wrote an article on the fifth anniversary of the second heist, saying it was a mystery that no sign of the money had ever been found. He also cast doubt on the identity of the Mexican. My father met with Rupert here in this very room and encouraged him to go to Mexico and try and find the grave of this mystery man.'

'And did he go?' asked Sarah.

'Yes, he did, about a year later. My father helped finance the trip.'

'And what did he find?'

Catherine looked out of the small window behind her father's desk and for a moment Frank thought that maybe she hadn't heard Sarah's question and was about to repeat the request. However, Sarah caught Frank's eye and raised a finger to her lips just as the attorney's daughter said, 'He never came back. My father received a disturbing letter saying that he had been buried alive, and that should he think of going to Reynosa, Mexico, the same would happen to him.'

'What did you father say to that?'

'It confirmed his suspicions that the Mexican was the key to solving the mystery. And that it would lead back to those who were involved and eventually the money.'

'But Don DeLuca is dead,' said Frank.

Sarah and Catherine remained silent.

'Well, isn't he?' asked Frank.

'That's what we are told to believe in the report that Dodd wrote for the Missouri Pacific Railroad,' said Catherine, 'Even though there is no record of a death certificate.'

'Do you think he could still be alive and living in Reynosa, Mexico?' asked Sarah.

'My father had his suspicions.'

Sarah shook her head. 'Oh dear, so what should we do now?'

'My father said to Rupert on leaving for Mexico, "Don't look for justice, just look for the money."'

With the light of the window behind her, Frank caught a glimpse of Fletcher in the strong features of this smart woman.

'You are your father's daughter,' he said. 'And I mean that as the sincerest of compliments.'

20

MEXICO

Going to Reynosa

Frank asked Sarah if she knew what she was asking.

Sarah was resolute. 'Yes,' she said. 'The three of us should go.'

'Too dangerous,' said Frank. 'I will go to Reynosa. You should stay and attend here. If Jenkins and Dodd come looking for me, just say that I have left but you don't know to where. Ned will protect you and your home.'

Ned nodded his approval.

Sarah held her breath as if in defiance and her cheeks puffed up and coloured. She exhaled in a huff. 'If you go on your own, you will be, will be,' she was getting agitated, 'will be buried alive.'

Ned looked concerned.

'If I do, I do. But better one than three.'

'If the three of us go, we can look out for each other.'

'Or all share the same grave,' said Frank sarcastically.

Sarah puffed up her cheeks again and this time when she exhaled it came out in a gush, a little like a train letting off steam. 'That has got to be better than living like this.'

Frank was getting annoyed. 'Living like what?' he snapped.

Sarah turned away and began to cry quietly, her body quivering.

Ned and Frank were both surprised by this sudden burst of emotion and were at a loss as to what to say or do. Finally,

Frank said, 'I apologize for my ill temper.'

Sarah turned slowly, wiping her eyes with a handkerchief taken from her sleeve. 'No, it's me. I am asking too much of life. I should be grateful for what I have and expect no more.'

Ned approached her. 'But what is it you expect, Sarah?'

Sarah dabbed at each eye and drew in a deep breath. 'I don't mean to be desperate for sympathy and companionship, but just look at me. Look at us. We live from hand-to-mouth and go hungry most of the time, and in a house that is falling down around our ears. And the winters! I'm sick of being cold all winter and it's been like this for a lifetime. Married too young, and to a weak man who ran away when it all got too hard. And me always wanting more, but this isn't living, we are just surviving day to day. Why can't it be better?'

Ned was silent and Frank followed his form.

'I want to be warm and I don't want to worry about when and where our next meal is coming from. But most of all, I want just a little dignity and respect. And I'm sick of looking and feeling ashamed.'

Ned tried to placate her. 'But I do respect you.' It came out like an appeal, though.

'I know that. You both do, more than I deserve when I carry on like this. But I want the sort of respect you get from neighbours and strangers when you walk down the street and look good, in fine clothes. Respect that comes from having a position within society where others can't dictate how the three of us should live our lives together. But to do that you need money, and I'm not talking about a handful of change, but real money.'

Frank and Ned dared not say a word, they just watched

and listened.

'When you are rich there are no rules. And you don't have to be smart or pretty when you've got real money in deep pockets. And out there somewhere is a fortune and if a Mexican named Don DeLuca can lead us to it, then we should go and find it. Together.'

Frank clasped both hands on top of his head and pursed his lips as if to stop from opening his mouth. He glanced at Ned who quickly averted his gaze. He looked back at Sarah. He had to speak.

'Sarah, this is a serious situation. Those who set me up were willing to let me hang to keep their secret. And even those who knew of the secret, like Davidson, lived in fear. And what if we all get down to Reynosa and walk into some sort of trap? Or worse.' Frank dropped his hands into his lap. 'Find nothing more than a grave.'

Sarah had regained her composure. 'If we find a grave, we find a grave.'

Frank looked to Ned then hard at Sarah. 'You and Ned deserve all and more, and if I could give it to you I would. But surely it's better to live here in Kansas than die in Mexico?'

Sarah's unyielding character had returned. 'No, it's not! I've had enough of this.' She tossed her head back. 'I would rather take my chances in Mexico with you two, than stay here and wonder for the rest of my days what might have been. We all take our chances in life. It's when we stop taking chances that we die inside.'

Frank lifted a hand onto the kitchen table and began to drum his fingers. 'What if the newspaper man had found DeLuca and was killed for doing so? That could happen to us.'

'But what if he found the truth?' She flicked the pages of her recipe book to view her notes. 'He must have found something, or why was a warning sent for others not to follow? And if Dodd and Jenkins did go to Lee's Summit to investigate Davidson's death, they know that you and an accomplice are searching for the same answers.'

'And those answers lie in Mexico,' said Frank in matter of fact acknowledgement.

Sarah nodded in silent agreement.

'How much money do we have?' asked Frank.

'Enough to get the three of us down to Mexico, but probably not enough to get back,' said Sarah.

'We may not need it,' whispered Frank under his breath.

'What was that?' asked Sarah.

'Oh, nothing. We can figure that out once we get there. Maybe we could do a little gold prospecting.' Frank looked up at Ned. 'What do you think, Ned? Should the three of us go to Mexico?'

'Yes,' said Ned with a clear purpose that surprised both Frank and Sarah. 'It is the three of us. I understand that now.'

The colour of Reynosa dust is yellow, just like the dust of the McAllen Ranch on the Texas side of the border. Only, somehow, just a little further south, on the Mexican side, it seems different. It glows in the light of the morning sun, just before the day heats up to the intensity of a blacksmith's furnace.

Their trip south had been without incident. The three travelled third class to San Antonio on the *Katy* and picked up the Southern Pacific to Alice before boarding a stage to McAllen's. From there they were in the hands of the

Mexicans and rode in an open wagon, pulled by mules, to Reynosa with a family of seven. Sarah kept notes in the back of her recipe book throughout the journey and wondered what state a body would be in if shipped from Kansas City to Reynosa in this simmering heat.

On arrival at Reynosa there was little relief to the eye from the hot arid landscape. The only accommodation they could find was at the back of a cantina called the Mexicali Rosa. In truth it was no more than converted stables where the stalls had been turned into small bunkrooms. But discomfort was the least of their problems. While the town's people seemed neither disagreeable nor agreeable, they had no way of communicating. No one admitted to speaking English and Sarah, Frank and Ned had no knowledge of the Spanish language.

They had agreed early on to be careful when asking questions where the name Don DeLuca was mentioned, as not to raise suspicion and reveal the reason for their visit. However, in the end, out of desperation, they started asking everyone, including the owner of the cantina.

'Don DeLuca?' said Sarah, raising her eyebrows in the hope that it would convey a question of his whereabouts.

The cantina owner had smiled and nodded at every question previously posed, but this time he gave a shrug of the shoulders and scowled.

'Was that a yes or no?' asked Frank.

Sarah was sure that she caught a slight shift in the owner's eyes. 'Shifty eyes are a tell-tale sign,' she said with authority.

'But still not an answer,' said Frank. 'Although, we may well have shown our hand, which may bring someone calling.'

It did: the town priest.

He was a tall and distinguished man with thick silver hair, a soft voice and polite manner. His English was perfect. Frank and Ned watched as he held Sarah's hand and charmed their senorita with his Mexican manner.

It was clear on both of their faces that they didn't much like his advances, priest or no priest.

'The family have all gone now,' he said. 'But tell me, how did you know of Señor Don DeLuca?'

'We believe that he passed away in Kansas and we are from Kansas,' said Sarah.

Sarah's response didn't make sense to Frank, but surprisingly, the priest seemed to accept her answer and nodded in agreement.

'Ah, yes, what a tragedy. Killed by a stray bullet. God rest his soul.'

'And his body was returned to Reynosa?'

'It was, where he now rests in peace. I officiated at his funeral myself.'

'And no family are left here in Reynosa?' asked Sarah, seeking clarification.

'No. None.'

The priest continued to hold Sarah's hand and she was now starting to feel a little uncomfortable. She pulled away with a gentle tug.

He held tight for a moment before releasing his grip to say, 'I'm sorry that you came so far for so little benefit.'

Sarah nodded and watched as the priest turned and walked to his buggy. As he was placing his foot on the step, she said, 'Could you show us where his body is buried?'

The priest stopped and lowered his foot to the ground but kept his back turned. However, Ned was standing to one side and caught sight of the holy man's face and noticed a scowl. Yet, on turning, the warm smile had returned.

'Of course, you should visit after coming all this way. His final resting place is in the small graveyard of the Chapel of Saint Leticia in the old town. The church is now unused and in disrepair, but I will show you. It is only two to three miles from here.'

Sarah hesitated then said, 'Thank you.'

Frank said, 'I'll come, too.'

'I'm sorry,' said the priest. 'My calesa is just for two people.'

Frank went to protest and was about to say that while it might be a bit of a squeeze, Sarah could sit—

Sarah interrupted his silent protest by saying, 'I'll be fine.'

Frank and Ned stood and watched the buggy with its two smart horses ride off in a swirl of yellow dust.

'That's a smart rig,' said Ned. 'It could take three at less than a jam. You could have gone along.'

Frank rubbed his chin. 'Is it me, Ned, or do you have an uneasy feeling about Sarah going off with a priest?'

'Should I?' asked Ned.

'No, you shouldn't, so why do I?'

'He's a bit all over her, isn't he? Holding her hand and up close. Is that what Mexican priests do?'

'I have no idea what goes on this side of the border, Ned. But it seems kind of odd to me.'

Sarah returned two hours later as the sun was setting and the light was turning the dust to gold.

'Did you see it?' asked Frank.

'I did. It was there just as he said. A little overgrown, but not that much. The name Don DeLuca is on the headstone, real clear.'

'So he is dead, then?'

Sarah paused and was looking at the priest in his depart-ing buggy. 'It would seem so,' she said in a reflective tone as if of two minds.

'You don't sound convinced,' said Frank.

'Don't I? I mean, I should, after all, he's a priest and he showed me the grave.'

Frank was hanging off every word but he was confused. It was as if Sarah was trying to say something without saying anything.

'I asked him about the newspaper man.'

Frank was surprised. 'You did? What did he say?'

'Said he had no knowledge of any such visit, but that it may have occurred while he was away doing missionary work.'

'Did you believe him?'

Sarah turned to look at Frank. 'Not for a minute.'

'Why?'

'We come all this way so that I can be shown, by an English speaking Mexican man of the cloth, the last resting place of Don DeLuca, a mystery man with no relatives in the town where he lived all his life.'

Sarah was calm and continued to speak softly and slowly. 'It's all so neat and pretty, isn't it? But life is never neat and pretty and it's certainly never damn convenient.'

Her cuss took Frank by surprise. 'So what do you think?'

'I think that a dead man, who was accidently shot by a stray bullet in a heist that never happened is not dead. And there is only one way to find out if this is all a contrivance.'

Frank was reluctant to ask, but he had to. 'How?'

'Dig up the grave,' came Sarah's curt response.

Frank's jaw dropped a little. 'What? You're joking, aren't you?'

Sarah was silent.

'Sarah?'

'Joking? No. Not really because I can't think of any other way. Can you?'

Now Frank fell silent.

'What about you, Ned?' asked Sarah.

Ned joined Frank in silence with his mouth also slightly open.

'Apparently not then. So give me a reason why we shouldn't go digging. Because I don't believe Don DeLuca is in that grave.'

21

IN A HOLE

The Chapel of Saint Leticia

It was Ned who acquired the three old flat bladed shovels with their long, worn handles. He had to use sign language to transact the purchase and spent almost all of the money they had left.

'We can sell them back,' said Sarah.

Frank wasn't convinced when he saw how years of use had smoothed the flat blades to a thin edge. 'I doubt if they will fetch or trade enough for a wagon ride back to McAllen's Ranch.'

Sarah took a small oil lamp from a hook on the back

wall of the cantina and told Ned to pocket the small red box of safety matches from the shelf. Then, with a shovel over her shoulder, she took off at a brisk pace. Frank and Ned followed her into the dark, but without half of Sarah's enthusiasm.

By the time they reached the small, dilapidated chapel it was close to midnight and with the aid of the lit lamp they were able to read the inscription on the headstone.

'It's him,' said Ned.

Frank stared down at the name Don DeLuca and was of two minds. One said leave the dead alone and go home, while the other said, well, we're here now so why not dig. Ned held back, not sure what to do. However, Sarah's intentions were clear as she commenced to roll up her sleeves.

Frank took off his jacket slowly and undid his belt to slide the old cavalry holster from his waist. He placed the handgun behind the headstone and hung his jacket over the top to hide the name before turning his cuffs to above the elbow. He sank the blade of the shovel into the earth and to his surprise, it was much softer than expected as the ground underfoot during Sarah's forced march to the old chapel was as hard as rock. Sarah joined in and with vigour scooped up a full blade of earth and deposited it onto Frank's foot.

'Let me start,' said Frank. 'Then Ned can follow. Then you. There is only room for one to dig at a time.'

Sarah reluctantly accepted the decree and stood back.

The periods of digging that followed were short but continuous as each stepped in and did their bit. Both Ned and Frank provided advice to Sarah on how to use the handle to lift a blade of soil from the pit onto the edge in one motion. And within the hour a large pile of earth was heaped to the left and right of the grave. This prompted Frank to suggest to Sarah that she stay topside and use her shovel to stop any of the soil from tumbling back into the dark void as he and Ned continued to dig.

Into the second hour, Frank found himself doing the lion's share of the work, but he did so willingly. While digging it allowed him to think and he came to the conclusion that Sarah was right. They had to know once and for all if this was the last resting place of Don DeLuca. And if it was, it could put to rest the suspicions and mystery they had assigned to this man. It would also end the Mexican connection to the heist and free them to go home to Kansas somehow, to face Jenkins and Dodd.

Sweat was now rolling from his forehead and dripping off the end of his nose as a small creek streamed down the furrow of his back, which made his shirt cling to the skin. It took the best part of the second hour before Frank's shovel struck the top of the casket. He scraped the upright blade upon the wooden surface and unexpectedly a chill passed through his body. His state of mind immediately switched to where it had been when he had started, which caused him to ask himself the question again. Is this right?

'You've reached it,' said Ned, on all fours and leaning down in the hope that he could see, but it was too dark. 'Deep,' he said. 'Do we pull it out or open it in there?'

'Shine the lamp,' said Frank.

Sarah handed the lamp to Ned who lowered it into the hole.

'You're standing on the coffin with nowhere to go. We will have to lift it out,' said Ned.

Frank tried to place a foot to either side of the narrow end of the box. 'Should have brought ropes,' he said.

'It hasn't rotted, has it?' asked Ned.

Frank tapped on the upper surface as if knocking on a door. 'Seems fine. Must be the dryness of the earth.'

'Maybe if we dig around the end, then we can lift it up with the shovel blades and slide it out,' said Ned.

'Worth a try,' said Frank.

'You hold the lamp,' said Ned to Sarah as he lifted his arm in her direction while still looking down at Frank.

But he received no reply.

He called again while leaning in a little further to look into the deep hole. 'Take the lamp, Sarah.'

But still there was no reply.

Ned pushed himself back from the edge of the open grave and lifted the lamp to illuminate the figure of Sarah, and immediately he let out a deep breath.

'What is it?' said Frank as he continued to brush the soil from the top of the coffin.

'Better come see,' said Ned quietly. 'We have company.'

'What company?' came the call from Frank as he stood up straight in an effort to look out over the edge of the grave. 'Can't see,' he said. 'Too much dirt.'

He placed the long handle of his shovel across the width of the open grave and used it as a perch to lift himself out and onto the edge while trying not to cause too much of the soil to spill back in. As he stood, he could see the fall of the light upon Sarah who was standing perfectly still with the upright shovel still in her hand. However, the look upon her face was that of alarm.

'What is it?' he repeated.

'It's the end, Frank,' came a voice. 'That's what it is.'

The light of the lamp only shone upon the lower half of the man who had spoken, showing just his boots and trouser legs. Frank knew that squeaky voice and Louisiana accent immediately. He had not heard it for twelve years, but it had never been forgotten. It could have been yesterday. It was Rodney D. Dodd.

Ned lifted the lamp for the light and it showed the figure of Dodd pointing a handgun that was being held close to his waist.

'I bet you're surprised,' Dodd said. 'Me being all the way down here to catch up with you.'

Frank was more than surprised; he was dumbfounded. He didn't know what to say as his mind raced to figure out how on earth Dodd could have possibly turned up, right here at this precise moment. But one thing he did know. They were in serious trouble. He glanced back down into the hole and then at Dodd.

'Convenient, isn't it?' remarked Dodd casually.

Stall-think-stall-think, came the voice inside Frank's head. But still he didn't know what to say. He just stood there with a silly look upon his face while his head swam in a sea of questions and not one answer.

Then, through the dark still night air came the sound of horses and clink of brass buckles.

'It's the priest,' said Sarah. She said it with a voice that is reserved for moments of salvation when unexpected rescue is close at hand.

The four of them all stood frozen to the spot as they heard the two horses come to the halt and the carriage springs squeak when the priest alighted.

'Over here, Father,' called Sarah.

Frank went to make a move, expecting Dodd to shift the aim of his revolver to Sarah as she made her call for help, but the barrel remained straight and true in Frank and Ned's direction.

With the sound of quick steps upon the path, the tall figure of the priest emerged out of the darkness and into the dim lamplight. He stopped and looked around before walking slowly towards Frank where he stopped again.

'When you disturb the final resting place of the deceased, you upset their loved ones,' he said.

'We can explain,' said Sarah.

The priest stepped forward to gaze into the open grave before looking back at Sarah. 'There is no need to explain, I know everything.'

'You do?' questioned Sarah.

'Yes. I don't need to know any more.' The priest turned to leave then paused and said, 'You came to meddle, when you should have stayed away and got on with your lives. As little as they are.'

Frank was astonished that the priest was about to leave and called, 'Father, you can't walk away. I know this man.' He nodded towards Dodd. 'If you leave, he will kill all three of us in cold blood. As a man of faith you can't have such an act upon your conscience.'

The priest slowly turned back to face Frank, but he said nothing.

Frank knew he had to plead and was willing to do so. 'This business is between me and this man, Dodd. Take the other two with you.'

Still the priest remained mute.

'At least let Sarah go with you.'

The priest turned towards Sarah and looked her up and down, but it was with a look of complete contempt. He then brushed her aside with a wave of the hand before advancing back towards Frank to address him up close, almost nose to nose.

'When I was first told about you, all those years ago, it was said that you were a fool and that you would never be able to work out what had happened. I listened, but doubted that it was true, so I made sure that our plan was not just believable but persuasive. It had to be more than just a duplication of your pathetic robbery.' The priest raised his hand and poked Frank in the chest. 'And I'll tell you why I doubted that you were a fool. You were never caught spending the money. That was your wisdom. My larceny was far bigger than your tiny ambitions, but I too spent my riches carefully and judiciously without being caught, while receiving life-long influence in return.' The priest's finger poked Frank in the chest again. 'When I heard that you had arrived here in Reynosa, I said to myself, you are smart. You have come to find the truth. Then, when I saw the three of you bumbling around, asking questions about Don DeLuca and buying shovels, I realized that Dodd had been right all along. You are nothing more than a fool who has dug his own grave, just like the newspaper man.' The look on the Mexican's face was a mix of fierce anger and savage pleasure. 'This is Mexico, and in Mexico your remains will never be found. You will die here, rot here, and remain here forever, and no one will ever know what happened to you.'

Frank felt a cold shudder run up the back of his spine. He had been a fool. No, worse. He had been the chief idiot who had dared to refer to others in such derogatory terms when he was the biggest idiot of all. But he would be a fool no more. At last he understood.

'You're not a priest, are you?' he said with cool calmness. 'You're Don DeLuca.'

'Once I was Don DeLuca. Now I am but a humble parish priest. It is my disguise for the stupid of this world.'

Ned spat upon the ground at DeLuca's feet while keeping his eyes on Dodd's pistol.

Sarah's lips opened slightly, but she remained mute as a sudden impulse came upon her. It was like a blast of heat from a furnace – a fusion of instinct and fury – a sensation she would be at a loss to explain after it had passed. But now trapped and confronted with her own mortality, Sarah refused to accept the inevitable. And with her instinct as a mother to care and protect those she loved, it became a force of dead reckoning.

She had, in one instantaneous and seamless motion, lifted and swung the heavy shovel in a wide sweeping arc. The blade flew through the air with such force that the handle now seemed to pull from her grip as if someone was trying to take the implement from her. This caused her to inadvertently roll her wrists so that the flat face of the shovel changed angles, and in doing so it became a lethal weapon like a large ancient axe, slicing through the dark night air at shoulder height and incredible speed.

The narrow steel edge of the spade struck the back of the Mexican's neck just below the base of the skull. The sound was sickening as the savage blow severed tissue, sliced muscle, and splintering bone. The head was flung back with such force that the snap of the neck was heard by all, except one. The Mexican.

If later, there was any regret in Sarah's mind for such a vicious and violent act, it was only that the blow from the thin steel blade was so precise as to cause no pain to the victim whatsoever. The Mexican was dead, but not by the means of the execution that he truly deserved.

As the top of the priest's spine severed, his body collapsed to the earth in a thud, as if by some act of a magician where every bone in his body had been removed by a magical wave of a wand. Dodd, who was in the best position to observe and witness the blow, reeled back in shock and surprise, to half stumble as his finger jerked upon the trigger. The wayward shot cracked through the air and hit the still raised blade of Sarah's shovel with a high pitched ping, making her drop it from her hands.

These unexpected actions and reactions provided the opportunity that allowed Frank and Ned to leap at Dodd with such speed that they failed to hear Sarah say with a gasp, 'Oh mercy, what have I done?'

Ned hit Dodd on the left side of the body and Frank made contact to the right almost at the same time. However, it was not a forceful blow from Frank as he too was falling to the ground. But as Dodd's legs buckled and he began to drop, the top of Frank's head went forward to smack hard into Dodd's nose, breaking bone and rendering him unconscious. As the three hit the ground, Frank and Ned immediately pulled back their arms with clenched fists to punch Dodd, but there was no need. The body was limp, so they both rolled onto their backs and looked up at the heavens with sheer relief.

'I think I've hurt the poor man,' said Sarah with concern as she looked down at the Mexican.

'Thankfully, yes,' said Frank.

'What should we do?' Sarah was kneeling and shaking the shoulder of a dead man. 'Will he wake up?'

Frank pulled himself up into the sitting position. 'Not on this earth but maybe someplace else.'

'Is it over?' asked Ned.

'Only if we can get to the other side of the border in one piece. To do that we need to get out of here fast and leave as little evidence behind as possible.'

Sarah prodded the Mexican's shoulder again. 'Should we bury him?'

Frank got up and walked over to the headstone and lifted his jacket to expose the name, Don DeLuca. 'Seems appropriate, this was supposed to be his last resting place and it may just give us the time we need.'

'What about Dodd?' said Ned.

Sarah looked over at the second body lying upon the ground. 'Is he dead?'

'No,' said Frank.

Sarah was fussing just a little. 'Do we take him with us?' she said as if questioning herself. 'We could tie him to the back of buggy, on the shelf.'

'First things first,' said Frank. 'We came to find out what was in this grave.'

'But it's not Don DeLuca,' said Sarah.

'No, it's not,' replied Frank.

Sarah pressed two fingers to her lips before she spoke. 'Then who?'

'I don't know,' said Frank. 'But I think it may be the newspaper man.'

'Oh, dear Lord,' said Sarah. 'I think we should let it be.'

'No,' said Frank. 'I was locked up by a lie and I now want to find out the truth, all of it. If it is the newspaper man, we can tell his family that we have found his last resting place. It will also implicate DeLuca and hopefully, Dodd and Jenkins.'

'Was he buried alive?' Sarah was now peering into the dark of the grave.

Frank stepped over the unconscious body of Dodd to stand beside her. 'So the letter to Attorney Prowse said.'

'What do you think, Ned?' asked Sarah.

Ned just shrugged.

'Come on, Ned,' said Frank. 'Let's get this over and done with so that we can go.'

The task that followed was not without its difficulties in removing the coffin from the grave in order to open the lid. At first, Frank tried to dig around the edges of the casket, but found that it was easier to insert the blade of his shovel under the foot of the box and ease it up. With a second shovel he was then able to hoist the narrow end of the coffin into the air, only to hear the disturbing sound of the contents shifting. By the time it was finally lifted free from the grave, with Frank and Ned both in the hole and pushing while Sarah guided it onto level ground, there was less than an hour left before the dawn.

It was Ned who suggested that they insert the blades of two shovels into the thin crack between the base of the coffin and the lid. With some frustrating effort as the blades kept slipping out, the lid finally started to move.

'Step away, Sarah,' said Frank, 'and avert your eyes.'

Sarah quickly did as she was told.

On the count of three and a final twist of the two shovels, the top of the coffin from the grave of Don DeLuca popped open and slid off to the side.

'Hold the lamp a little higher, Sarah, but don't come any closer.'

Sarah lifted the lamp high and edged forward just a little. The lid that now rested upright on its side and against the coffin hid her view of the contents.

'Good Lord,' said Ned. 'Will you look at that?'

Frank let out a long low whistle. 'I'm looking, Ned, but I'm not believing. Are you?'

'No, I'm not. Who would have thought?'

'What is it?' asked Sarah.

'You better come and see,' said Frank.

'I don't know,' said Sarah hesitantly.

'I think you should,' said Ned.

Slowly she stepped forward with the lamp held high as it chased away the shadows from the open casket to reveal a mass of paper money and the glitter of three gold bars.

'Oh my, where did that come from?'

Frank pulled a mailbag from the foot of the coffin with MPR stencilled in large letters. 'This is the money from the robbery that I served twelve years for.'

'Oh my,' said Sarah again. 'Then it's your money, Frank. Every last penny of it.'

'Well, it certainly isn't Don DeLuca's any more,' said Frank.

Sarah knelt and lifted one of the heavy gold bars. 'Was this part of the robbery?'

'I don't know,' said Frank, 'but it's ours now.'

Sarah ran her hands through the mass of notes, before picking up the large mailbag and opening it wide.

'Ned,' she called. 'Start shovelling it in so that Frank can see the size of his fortune.'

'Not my fortune,' corrected Frank. 'Our fortune.'

When the coffin was emptied and placed back in the grave, the body of Don DeLuca was dropped into the box without ceremony or care, to rest where the headstone had predicted all those years before.

Frank said quietly, 'Ned, will you take Sarah to the buggy and secure the mailbag ready for our departure?'

Sarah began protesting. 'I can still help and shovel in the soil.'

But Ned's firm grip upon her arm told her that she should do as she was told. When they got to the buggy, Ned quickly began to secure the bag under the bench seat, saying, 'Just keep pushing it in until it is completely under and secure.'

It was just a moment later that a single shot from a handgun broke the still silence.

Sarah jumped with a start while Ned just kept talking. 'Just keep pushing. Nearly there.'

When the bag was firmly in place, Ned said, 'Jump up and get ready to leave. I'll give Frank a hand to clean up.'

Sarah sat and waited as the first light of the day started to turn the dust to the colour of gold. When Ned and Frank returned, she could see the handle of Dodd's pistol protruding from Frank's pocket and next to his holster.

'Let's go,' said Frank as he slid onto the bench seat next to Sarah and Ned, and kicked the heel of his boot against the bulging mailbag for good measure.

But Sarah held tight to the reins and kept the buggy still.

'What are we waiting for, Sarah?' said Frank.

'I need to know.'

Frank knew what was coming, but he still asked, 'Need to know what?'

'Did you kill Dodd and bury his body with the Mexican?'

'Yes,' said Frank.

'Did you have to?'

'Yes,' said Frank. 'I wasn't going to spend the rest of my life waiting for him to come after me. We have the riches to start a new life on our terms and with Dodd and DeLuca dead, Jenkins will now live in fear that I will come after him. I did what I did and will have to live with it. I've never killed a man before.'

'Nor me,' said Sarah quietly. 'So we are now bound by a terrible secret.'

'Yes,' said Frank, 'but one we can manage. When you are rich, very rich, you can buy silence and bury your secrets deep. And we are now rich, very rich.'

'It is our bond,' confirmed Ned.

'Yes,' said Sarah with a smile of relief. 'It is our bond, Ned, and it will hold the three of us together forever.' With a quick flick of the reins from her tightly clenched fingers, the buggy of the Mexican lurched forwards into a trot towards the border.

22

THE RECITAL

1900, Stilwell, Kansas

The parlour held an audience of neighbours and acquaintances. The women were in their finest and had each been presented with an orchid corsage, while the men were in their Sunday suits and feigning interest. All were seated upon the well-upholstered French furniture as they sipped English tea from the finest of china cups and admired their surroundings. They were many but the room was not over crowded, it was much too large for that, even with the highly polished rosewood Rococo Steinway grand piano front and centre.

'From New York,' said Mrs Boetticher, pointing her eyes to the magnificent musical instrument. Mrs Kennedy was impressed while Mr Ballard looked on and gave a stern nod of approval. 'Paid for in cash and shipped out in a special container on the Missouri Pacific with a piano tuner,' continued Mrs Boetticher with her chin bouncing up and down in fierce agreement with her announcement.

'The opulence,' said Mrs Kennedy.

'The money,' questioned Mr Ballard. 'Just where did you get the sort of money to do something like that?'

'A gold mine in Mexico,' said Mrs Boetticher, who had become somewhat of an expert on the matter after her re-acquaintance with Sarah. 'Or so I've been told.' Mrs Boetticher lowered her voice. 'Sarah, Edward and Francis went there to find a missing man, and while there they stumbled upon an old gold lease and did some prospecting on the side. Even Sarah was on the end of a shovel. She told me so, and struck it rich.'

'I should be so lucky,' said Mr Ballard. 'Did they find the man they were looking for?'

Mrs Boetticher put her lips to the cup before lamenting, 'Alas, no.'

'Are they going back to look again?' Mr Ballard's manner was abrupt at the best of times and drinking tea had made it more so.

'No,' said Mrs Boetticher. 'Unfortunately he is a lost soul.'

'Don't blame them. Dangerous down there. People disappear all the time with never a trace to be found. That's where the bad lands are nowadays. Do you remember when Senator Jenkins went down there to find that man Dodd who worked for him? Returned without so much as a word.'

'Sad,' lamented Mrs Kennedy.

'Mind you, Jenkins couldn't find his way around a barn if it had more than two stalls. He's done nothing for the people of Topeka. They'll vote him out this next election unless he can do some pork barrelling. Word also has it that his campaign funds have dried up.'

Mrs Ballard, a small thin woman, who had been sitting quietly and listening to her husband, leant in toward Mrs Boetticher. 'Dear, what are the arrangements?'

Mrs Ballard immediately realized that she would have to explain her question and gave a slight cough, then said, 'Are they all living together under the same roof?'

Mrs Boetticher straightened her back. 'It is a big house, very big house, with separate bedrooms and with access to separate ablutions. I believe it is more like a boarding house than a mansion.'

'Still, it seems a little odd, doesn't it?'

Mrs Boetticher rode to the defence. 'Not at all. These are modern times, a new century, with a new design in housing, and it has come to Kansas. I mean, you could spend a week going from room to room and not run into another person other than the house staff.'

Mr Kennedy wasn't interested in the gossip. 'I prefer coffee to tea,' he said.

Mrs Boetticher was pleased to change the subject as her own quiet thoughts on the particular matter under discussion had, at times, given over to misgivings. However, the generous financial loan from Sarah for Robert Boetticher Junior to attend medical school in Boston had rusted her loyalty in place.

'They have brandy wine from France,' she added willingly. 'For medicinal purposes.'

Albert Kennedy's eyes lit up. 'They do?' He caught Ned's eye then called in a loud whisper, 'Ned, do you have brandy here? I feel a chill coming on.'

Frank was on his feet and patted Ned's shoulder to show that he would look after it. When he got to the small group he spoke quietly into Albert's ear, 'How bad is the chill, Bert?'

Albert started to relent. 'Not really that bad.'

'Pity, because I've got some Kentucky corn. Been lying on charcoal oak for ten years, but it's only for the prevention of real bad chills.'

Albert coughed. 'Mine could be bad.'

'Sounds bad. One or two fingers.'

'How long is the recital?'

'Long.'

'Better make it three.'

'I'll make it four so that you can forget about the bum notes.'

'Four, and I'll forget about anything you want me to.'

'That's normally how I find it works too,' said Frank, but Albert Kennedy didn't hear Frank's response as the applause drowned out all of the conversation in the room.

Sarah had entered the opulent parlour and seemed to magically float across the gleaming floor to take up her position before the piano. As she sat the folds of her elegant silk tea gown rustled then gently ballooned into the perfect shape of a bell.

Frank went to resume his seat but Albert grabbed his arm.

'Frank, we need to talk. I have a business proposition for you. It's about quality horse stock for a stud. Everything is ready to go. All we need is the capital. Interested?'

'Always interested in doing business, Bert. Especially with friends and neighbours, or how else is a man going to stay rich and happy?'

Albert winked at Frank. 'Right, you're absolutely right, friend and neighbour. We need to stick together and protect each other. Particularly from those blasted politicians, bureaucrats and lawyers in the capitol. They'll put you in an early grave if they get half a chance.'

Frank winked at Albert and gave a confident and relaxed smile. 'To that I can attest.'

Sarah straightened her back, took in a deep breath, held it for a moment then pounced upon the ivory keys to the opening notes of 'Chopsticks'. Her debut recital had begun.